Spectres and Souffles

Excerpt

The bells above the door jangled as Sabrina Spellsworth whirled behind the counter of the Crossroads Diner, her vintage polka-dot dress swishing around her knees. She deftly balanced plates laden with steaming comfort food, delivering them to the booths with a dazzling smile.

Two orders of meatloaf with extra gravy, one spectral cobb salad, hold the ectoplasm, she thought, mentally ticking off the orders. Sabrina moved with fluid grace, sidestepping the occasional ghostly patron who drifted through the bustling diner.

As she poured a cup of coffee for a translucent gentleman reading a newspaper from the 1920s, a new customer slid onto a stool at the counter. The middle-aged woman had a perplexed expression as she surveyed the eclectic mix of patrons, both corporeal and incorporeal.

"Welcome to the Crossroads Diner," Sabrina greeted warmly, setting a menu in front of the woman. "What can I get started for you today?"

The woman hesitated, her eyes darting to a nearby table where a ghostly couple shared a sundae, their spoons passing through each other. "I'm sorry, but... am I seeing things, or are some of your customers a bit... otherworldly?"

Sabrina chuckled, leaning conspiratorially across the counter. "Oh, you're not seeing things, sugar. The Crossroads Diner is a special place where the living and the dead can mingle over a good cup of joe and some home cooking."

The woman's eyes widened. "And you can... see them? Talk to them?"

"Sure can," Sabrina winked. "It's a gift I've had since I was a little girl. Now, it's my mission to make sure everyone feels welcome here, no matter which side of the veil they're on."

As if on cue, a spectral waitress glided past, her form shimmering as she carried a tray of ethereal entrées. The woman watched in amazement, then turned back to Sabrina.

"That's incredible! How do you manage it all?"

Sabrina shrugged, a mischievous glint in her eye. "Oh, you know, a little bit of intuition, a dash of empathy, and a whole lot of strong coffee. Speaking of which, can I interest you in a cup?"

The woman nodded, a smile spreading across her face. "You know what? I think I will. And maybe one of those famous cherry pies I've heard so much about."

"Coming right up," Sabrina grinned, already reaching for the coffee pot. As she poured, she couldn't help but feel a sense of pride and purpose. *The Crossroads Diner may be a bit unconventional,* she thought, *but it's exactly where I'm meant to be.*

As Sabrina handed the woman her coffee and a generous slice of cherry pie, a sudden chill ran down her spine. She turned to see a ghostly figure hovering near the end of the counter, frantically waving its ethereal arms to get her attention.

That's odd, Sabrina thought, furrowing her brow. *Usually, the spirits here are pretty laid back. Something must be up.*

Excusing herself from the conversation with the curious customer, Sabrina made her way to the far end of the counter, where the agitated spirit awaited. As she approached, the ghost leaned in close, its whispered words sending a tingle through her body.

"Sabrina, you won't believe it," the spirit hissed, its translucent eyes wide with excitement. "There's a new arrival in the spirit realm, and he's causing quite a stir among the other ghosts!"

Sabrina's heart skipped a beat. "A new arrival? Who is it? What's going on?"

The ghost glanced around furtively, as if afraid of being overheard. "I don't have all the details yet, but apparently, this newcomer is shaking things up in a big way. You might want to look into it."

With that, the spirit vanished, leaving Sabrina alone with her thoughts. She bit her lip, her curiosity piqued by the tantalizing tidbit of information. *A new spirit causing a commotion? This could be interesting...*

Spectres and Souffles

Glancing around the diner to ensure everything was running smoothly, Sabrina slipped away from the counter and made her way to a secluded corner booth. She slid into the seat, closing her eyes and focusing her energy on the spirit realm.

Alright, whoever you are, she thought, reaching out with her mind. *Let's see what all the fuss is about.*

As she concentrated, the diner around her faded away, replaced by a shimmering, ethereal landscape. Sabrina felt a presence nearby, the same ghostly patron who had delivered the mysterious message.

"Okay, spill," Sabrina said, her voice echoing in the otherworldly space. "Who's this new arrival, and why is everyone so worked up about them?"

The ghost materialized before her, its form solidifying as it prepared to divulge the juicy details. Sabrina leaned forward, her eyes sparkling with anticipation, ready to unravel the mystery of the spirit realm's newest resident.

The ghostly patron, a portly man with a handlebar mustache, took a deep breath before speaking. "Well, you see, the new arrival is none other than Chef François Dupont, the world-renowned culinary genius."

Sabrina's eyebrows shot up. "Wait, THE Chef Dupont? The one with three Michelin stars and a reality TV show?"

The ghost nodded solemnly. "The very same. But here's the thing—he's not content with just being a spirit. No, no. He's determined to elevate the diner's menu from comfort food to haute cuisine!"

Sabrina's jaw dropped. "He wants to do what now? This is a classic American diner, not some fancy-schmancy restaurant!"

The ghost shrugged. "Try telling him that. He's been floating around the kitchen, critiquing everything from the burger patties to the pie crusts. He even possessed one of the line cooks and made them whip up a 'deconstructed' grilled cheese sandwich."

Oh, for the love of all things deep-fried and delicious, Sabrina thought, rubbing her temples. *This is the last thing I need right now.*

"Thank you for the heads up," she said to the ghostly patron. "I'll handle it from here."

As the spirit realm faded away and the diner came back into focus, Sabrina found herself back in the corner booth, her mind reeling with the news. She drummed her fingers on the table, contemplating her next move.

If Chef Dupont thinks he can just waltz in here and start changing things, he's got another thing coming, she mused, her resolve hardening. *This is my diner, and I'll be damned if I let some hoity-toity ghost disrupt the harmony we've got going on here.*

With a nod, Sabrina slid out of the booth and straightened her apron. It was time to investigate the situation further and put a stop to Chef Dupont's culinary meddling before things got out of hand.

As Sabrina made her way back to the counter, she couldn't help but chuckle at the sight of Mort Grimshaw, the resident grim reaper, perched on a stool with his bony elbows resting on the formica surface. He was engrossed in a game of chess with a ghostly patron, his scythe leaning casually against the counter.

"Well, well, well, if it isn't the Reaper himself," Sabrina quipped, sliding behind the counter. "I thought you were supposed to be on sabbatical, Mort."

Mort glanced up from the chessboard, his eye sockets glowing with amusement. "Even death takes a holiday, my dear. Besides, where else can I find such stimulating company and a decent cup of coffee?"

Sabrina laughed, pouring him a fresh cup of joe. "Flattery will get you everywhere, Mort. But I'm afraid I need to ask for a favor."

"Oh?" Mort arched a non-existent eyebrow. "Do tell."

Sabrina leaned in conspiratorially. "We've got a new arrival in the spirit realm, a celebrity chef named François Dupont. He's causing quite a stir in the kitchen, trying to change up the menu and possession-hopping like it's going out of style."

Mort took a sip of his coffee, his skeletal grin widening. "Ah, yes, I've heard of Monsieur Dupont. Quite the culinary legend, or so he believes. What do you need from me, Sabrina?"

"I was hoping you could help me deal with him," Sabrina said, her hazel eyes pleading. "You know the ins and outs of the afterlife better than anyone. Maybe you could talk some sense into him, convince him to tone down the gourmet antics?"

Spectres and Souffles

Ghostly Recipes for the Haunted Kitchen

1. Phantom's Fog Soup

Ingredients:

- 1 head of cauliflower, chopped
- 1 white onion, diced
- 2 cloves of garlic, minced
- 4 cups vegetable broth
- 1/2 cup heavy cream
- 2 tbsp butter
- Salt and white pepper to taste
- Dry ice (for serving)

Instructions:

1. In a large pot, sauté onions and garlic in butter until translucent.
2. Add cauliflower and vegetable broth. Simmer until cauliflower is tender.
3. Blend the mixture until smooth.
4. Stir in cream and season with salt and white pepper.
5. Serve in black bowls. Just before serving, add a small piece of dry ice to create a ghostly fog effect. (Caution: Do not consume dry ice!)

2. Witch's Fingers Breadsticks

Ingredients:

- 2 cups all-purpose flour
- 1 tsp salt
- 1 tsp sugar
- 1 packet active dry yeast

- 3/4 cup warm water
- 2 tbsp olive oil
- Green food coloring
- Sliced almonds for fingernails

Instructions:

1. Mix flour, salt, sugar, and yeast in a bowl.
2. Add warm water and olive oil. Knead until smooth.
3. Add green food coloring for a sickly hue. Knead until color is even.
4. Let dough rise for 1 hour.
5. Shape dough into finger-like breadsticks. Press an almond slice at one end for a nail.
6. Bake at 375°F (190°C) for 12-15 minutes until golden brown.

3. Graveyard Dirt Pudding Cups

Ingredients:

- 1 package chocolate instant pudding
- 2 cups cold milk
- 1 package chocolate sandwich cookies, crushed
- Gummy worms
- Milano cookies
- Black decorating gel

Instructions:

1. Prepare pudding according to package instructions.
2. In clear cups, layer pudding and crushed cookies to resemble dirt.
3. Stick half a Milano cookie into each cup to represent a tombstone.
4. Write "RIP" on each tombstone with black gel.
5. Add gummy worms, partially buried in the "dirt".
6. Refrigerate until ready to serve.

4. Bloody Mary Tomato Soup

Ingredients:

- 2 cans whole peeled tomatoes
- 1 onion, chopped
- 2 cloves garlic, minced
- 2 cups vegetable broth
- 1/4 cup vodka (optional)
- 2 tbsp Worcestershire sauce
- 1 tsp hot sauce
- Salt and pepper to taste
- Celery sticks and olives for garnish

Instructions:

1. Sauté onion and garlic until soft.
2. Add tomatoes, broth, vodka, Worcestershire sauce, and hot sauce. Simmer for 20 minutes.
3. Blend until smooth. Season with salt and pepper.
4. Serve in glasses rimmed with celery salt. Garnish with a celery stick and olives on a skewer.

5. Mummy's Hand Meatloaf

Ingredients:

- 2 lbs ground beef
- 1 cup breadcrumbs
- 2 eggs
- 1 onion, finely chopped
- 1 tsp garlic powder
- Salt and pepper to taste
- Ketchup
- Sliced cheese

Spectres and Souffles

- Sliced olives

Instructions:

1. Mix beef, breadcrumbs, eggs, onion, garlic powder, salt, and pepper.
2. Shape the mixture into a hand shape on a baking sheet.
3. Bake at 350°F (175°C) for 50 minutes.
4. Cut cheese into thin strips and arrange over the meatloaf like bandages.
5. Use sliced olives for fingernails and eyes.
6. Drizzle ketchup for a bloody effect.
7. Bake for an additional 10 minutes until cheese melts.

Patti Petrone Miller

Copyright © [2024 by Patti Petrone Miller

All rights reserved.

No part of this publication may be reproduced, distributed, or transmitted in any form or by any means, including photocopying, recording, or other electronic or mechanical methods, without the prior written permission of the publisher.

The story, all names, characters, and incidents portrayed in this production are fictitious. No identification with actual persons (living or deceased), places, buildings, and products is intended or should be inferred.

Book Cover by TMT Book Cover Designs

1 edition 2024

Spectres and Souffles

by Patti Petrone Miller

Patti Petrone Miller

For my puppies
Tessa, Elliot, Brutus, Sam, Penny, Sophie, Jack, and Trixie

For Harold...

Spectres and Souffles

Chapter 1

The bells above the door jangled as Sabrina Spellsworth whirled behind the counter of the Crossroads Diner, her vintage polka-dot dress swishing around her knees. She deftly balanced plates laden with steaming comfort food, delivering them to the booths with a dazzling smile.

Two orders of meatloaf with extra gravy, one spectral cobb salad, hold the ectoplasm, she thought, mentally ticking off the orders. Sabrina moved with fluid grace, sidestepping the occasional ghostly patron who drifted through the bustling diner.

As she poured a cup of coffee for a translucent gentleman reading a newspaper from the 1920s, a new customer slid onto a stool at the counter. The middle-aged woman had a perplexed expression as she surveyed the eclectic mix of patrons, both corporeal and incorporeal.

"Welcome to the Crossroads Diner," Sabrina greeted warmly, setting a menu in front of the woman. "What can I get started for you today?"

The woman hesitated, her eyes darting to a nearby table where a ghostly couple shared a sundae, their spoons passing through each other. "I'm sorry, but... am I seeing things, or are some of your customers a bit... otherworldly?"

Sabrina chuckled, leaning conspiratorially across the counter. "Oh, you're not seeing things, sugar. The Crossroads Diner is a special place where the living and the dead can mingle over a good cup of joe and some home cooking."

The woman's eyes widened. "And you can... see them? Talk to them?"

"Sure can," Sabrina winked. "It's a gift I've had since I was a little girl. Now, it's my mission to make sure everyone feels welcome here, no matter which side of the veil they're on."

As if on cue, a spectral waitress glided past, her form shimmering as she carried a tray of ethereal entrées. The woman watched in amazement, then turned back to Sabrina.

"That's incredible! How do you manage it all?"

Sabrina shrugged, a mischievous glint in her eye. "Oh, you know, a little bit of intuition, a dash of empathy, and a whole lot of strong coffee. Speaking of which, can I interest you in a cup?"

The woman nodded, a smile spreading across her face. "You know what? I think I will. And maybe one of those famous cherry pies I've heard so much about."

"Coming right up," Sabrina grinned, already reaching for the coffee pot. As she poured, she couldn't help but feel a sense of pride and purpose. *The Crossroads Diner may be a bit unconventional,* she thought, *but it's exactly where I'm meant to be.*

As Sabrina handed the woman her coffee and a generous slice of cherry pie, a sudden chill ran down her spine. She turned to see a ghostly figure hovering near the end of the counter, frantically waving its ethereal arms to get her attention.

That's odd, Sabrina thought, furrowing her brow. *Usually, the spirits here are pretty laid back. Something must be up.*

Excusing herself from the conversation with the curious customer, Sabrina made her way to the far end of the counter, where the agitated spirit awaited. As she approached, the ghost leaned in close, its whispered words sending a tingle through her body.

"Sabrina, you won't believe it," the spirit hissed, its translucent eyes wide with excitement. "There's a new arrival in the spirit realm, and he's causing quite a stir among the other ghosts!"

Sabrina's heart skipped a beat. "A new arrival? Who is it? What's going on?"

The ghost glanced around furtively, as if afraid of being overheard. "I don't have all the details yet, but apparently, this newcomer is shaking things up in a big way. You might want to look into it."

With that, the spirit vanished, leaving Sabrina alone with her thoughts. She bit her lip, her curiosity piqued by the tantalizing tidbit of information. *A new spirit causing a commotion? This could be interesting...*

Glancing around the diner to ensure everything was running smoothly, Sabrina slipped away from the counter and made her way to a secluded corner booth. She slid into the seat, closing her eyes and focusing her energy on the spirit realm.

Alright, whoever you are, she thought, reaching out with her mind. *Let's see what all the fuss is about.*

As she concentrated, the diner around her faded away, replaced by a shimmering, ethereal landscape. Sabrina felt a presence nearby, the same ghostly patron who had delivered the mysterious message.

"Okay, spill," Sabrina said, her voice echoing in the otherworldly space. "Who's this new arrival, and why is everyone so worked up about them?"

The ghost materialized before her, its form solidifying as it prepared to divulge the juicy details. Sabrina leaned forward, her eyes sparkling with anticipation, ready to unravel the mystery of the spirit realm's newest resident.

The ghostly patron, a portly man with a handlebar mustache, took a deep breath before speaking. "Well, you see, the new arrival is none other than Chef François Dupont, the world-renowned culinary genius."

Sabrina's eyebrows shot up. "Wait, THE Chef Dupont? The one with three Michelin stars and a reality TV show?"

The ghost nodded solemnly. "The very same. But here's the thing—he's not content with just being a spirit. No, no. He's determined to elevate the diner's menu from comfort food to haute cuisine!"

Sabrina's jaw dropped. "He wants to do what now? This is a classic American diner, not some fancy-schmancy restaurant!"

The ghost shrugged. "Try telling him that. He's been floating around the kitchen, critiquing everything from the burger patties to the pie crusts. He even possessed one of the line cooks and made them whip up a 'deconstructed' grilled cheese sandwich."

Oh, for the love of all things deep-fried and delicious, Sabrina thought, rubbing her temples. *This is the last thing I need right now.*

"Thank you for the heads up," she said to the ghostly patron. "I'll handle it from here."

Spectres and Souffles

As the spirit realm faded away and the diner came back into focus, Sabrina found herself back in the corner booth, her mind reeling with the news. She drummed her fingers on the table, contemplating her next move.

If Chef Dupont thinks he can just waltz in here and start changing things, he's got another thing coming, she mused, her resolve hardening. *This is my diner, and I'll be damned if I let some hoity-toity ghost disrupt the harmony we've got going on here.*

With a nod, Sabrina slid out of the booth and straightened her apron. It was time to investigate the situation further and put a stop to Chef Dupont's culinary meddling before things got out of hand.

As Sabrina made her way back to the counter, she couldn't help but chuckle at the sight of Mort Grimshaw, the resident grim reaper, perched on a stool with his bony elbows resting on the formica surface. He was engrossed in a game of chess with a ghostly patron, his scythe leaning casually against the counter.

"Well, well, well, if it isn't the Reaper himself," Sabrina quipped, sliding behind the counter. "I thought you were supposed to be on sabbatical, Mort."

Mort glanced up from the chessboard, his eye sockets glowing with amusement. "Even death takes a holiday, my dear. Besides, where else can I find such stimulating company and a decent cup of coffee?"

Sabrina laughed, pouring him a fresh cup of joe. "Flattery will get you everywhere, Mort. But I'm afraid I need to ask for a favor."

"Oh?" Mort arched a non-existent eyebrow. "Do tell."

Sabrina leaned in conspiratorially. "We've got a new arrival in the spirit realm, a celebrity chef named François Dupont. He's causing quite a stir in the kitchen, trying to change up the menu and possession-hopping like it's going out of style."

Mort took a sip of his coffee, his skeletal grin widening. "Ah, yes, I've heard of Monsieur Dupont. Quite the culinary legend, or so he believes. What do you need from me, Sabrina?"

"I was hoping you could help me deal with him," Sabrina said, her hazel eyes pleading. "You know the ins and outs of the afterlife better than anyone. Maybe you could talk some sense into him, convince him to tone down the gourmet antics?"

Mort chuckled darkly, setting down his coffee cup. "You want me to play mediator between a stubborn ghost chef and a living world diner? Oh, this should be interesting."

Please say yes, Sabrina thought, biting her lip. *I don't know if I can handle this on my own.*

Mort studied Sabrina for a moment, his gaze inscrutable. Then, with a dramatic sigh, he pushed himself off the stool and grabbed his scythe. "Very well, my dear. I suppose I can't let you face this culinary crisis alone. Lead the way to the kitchen, and let's see if we can't persuade Chef Dupont to embrace the beauty of comfort food."

Sabrina beamed, relief flooding through her. "Thank you, Mort. You're a lifesaver. Or, well, a death-saver, I guess."

Mort snorted, his eye sockets twinkling with mirth. "Just don't expect me to don an apron and start flipping burgers. I have a reputation to uphold, you know."

Of course, Sabrina mused, suppressing a grin. *Heaven forbid the Grim Reaper gets caught dead in a diner uniform.*

With Mort by her side, Sabrina felt a renewed sense of determination as they made their way towards the kitchen, ready to confront the ghostly chef and protect the beloved Crossroads Diner from his haute cuisine ambitions.

As they approached the kitchen, Sabrina's mind raced with possible strategies to convince Chef François to embrace the diner's traditional menu. She glanced at Mort, hoping his otherworldly wisdom might provide some guidance.

Maybe we could appeal to his sense of nostalgia, she mused. *Remind him of the simple joys of classic diner fare.*

Mort, as if sensing her thoughts, leaned in and whispered, "Remember, Sabrina, diplomacy is key. We don't want to ruffle any ghostly feathers, especially those of a temperamental chef."

Sabrina nodded, taking a deep breath as they entered the kitchen. The sight that greeted them was one of controlled chaos. Ghostly line cooks darted about, their movements a blur as they prepared dishes that looked more at home in a Michelin-starred restaurant than a humble diner.

In the center of it all stood Chef François, his translucent form commanding attention as he barked orders in a heavy French accent.

"Non, non, non! The presentation must be perfect! We are not serving slop to the masses!"

Sabrina cleared her throat, catching the chef's attention. "Chef François, may we have a word?"

The ghostly chef whirled around, his eyes narrowing as he took in Sabrina and Mort. "Ah, the proprietress and her macabre companion. What brings you to my domain?"

His domain? Sabrina thought, trying to keep her annoyance in check. *Last I checked, this was still my diner.*

"We were hoping to discuss the menu changes," Sabrina began, her tone carefully measured. "While we appreciate your culinary expertise, we feel that the diner's traditional fare is an integral part of its charm."

Chef François scoffed, waving a dismissive hand. "Charm? You call greasy burgers and limp fries charm? No, no, my dear. I am elevating this establishment to new heights of gastronomic excellence!"

Mort stepped forward, his scythe glinting under the fluorescent lights. "Now, listen here, Chef. I've been around long enough to know that sometimes, the simplest things in life (and death) are the most satisfying. There's a reason why souls keep coming back to this diner, and it's not for the fancy plating."

The ghostly chef bristled, his form flickering with indignation. "You dare question my vision? I am Chef François Dupont, culinary legend!"

Time for a different approach, Sabrina thought, inspiration striking. "Chef François, what if we found a way to incorporate your talents without completely overhauling the menu? Perhaps you could create a few signature dishes that complement our classic offerings."

Mort nodded, catching on to Sabrina's plan. "A compromise, if you will. A chance to showcase your skills while still honoring the diner's legacy."

Chef François paused, considering their proposal. "A compromise, you say? Hmm, I suppose I could lend my expertise to elevate a few select dishes. But I will not be held responsible for the pedestrian palates of your patrons!"

Sabrina fought back a smile, sensing victory within reach. "Of course, Chef. We would be honored to have your special touches on our menu."

As Chef François turned back to his ghostly brigade, muttering about the concessions he was forced to make, Sabrina and Mort exchanged a triumphant glance.

Crisis averted, Sabrina thought, relief washing over her. *Now, let's just hope his signature dishes don't involve ectoplasm or ghostly garnishes.*

With the kitchen drama resolved (for now), Sabrina and Mort made their way back to the diner floor, ready to face whatever supernatural challenges the Crossroads Diner had in store for them next.

As Sabrina and Mort emerged from the kitchen, the diner's patrons were abuzz with curiosity. Ethereal whispers mingled with the clinking of silverware, as both living and deceased customers speculated about the commotion they'd overheard.

"What was all that racket about?" asked Gladys, a regular ghost who'd been frequenting the diner since the 1950s. "Sounded like someone was stirring up trouble in the kitchen."

Sabrina smiled reassuringly, her hazel eyes sparkling with mischief. "Oh, just a little culinary debate, Gladys. Nothing to worry about. In fact, I think you'll be pleasantly surprised by some new additions to the menu."

Gladys raised a translucent eyebrow, intrigued. "New additions, you say? Well, as long as you're not messing with my favorite cherry pie recipe, I suppose I can keep an open mind."

If only she knew, Sabrina thought, suppressing a chuckle. *Chef François would probably consider that cherry pie a crime against pastry.*

Mort, who had been silently observing the exchange, leaned in closer to Sabrina. "You know, I've got to hand it to you, Spellsworth. You've got a knack for diffusing supernatural situations with that charm of yours."

Sabrina grinned, playfully elbowing the grim reaper. "What can I say, Mort? It's all part of the job description when you run a diner that caters to the living and the dead."

Spectres and Souffles

As the duo made their rounds, checking on customers and ensuring everything was running smoothly, Sabrina couldn't help but feel a sense of pride. The Crossroads Diner was more than just a restaurant; it was a sanctuary where two worlds could collide and coexist in harmony.

And with a little luck and a lot of diplomacy, Sabrina mused, *we might just be able to keep it that way... even with a ghostly gourmet shaking things up in the kitchen.*

Little did Sabrina know, the culinary adventures with Chef François were only the beginning of the otherworldly antics that awaited her at the Crossroads Diner.

Chef François waved his hand dismissively, his translucent form shimmering under the fluorescent lights of the kitchen. "Ma chère, while I appreciate your... concerns, I must insist that this menu requires a significant upgrade. The palette of the afterlife demands more than just greasy burgers and bland fries."

Sabrina raised an eyebrow, her lips twitching with a hint of amusement. "Chef François, I understand your passion for haute cuisine, but our customers come to the Crossroads Diner for comfort food and a welcoming atmosphere. It's what keeps them coming back, both the living and the dead."

The ghostly chef scoffed, his spectral toque blanche quivering with indignation. "Mademoiselle Spellsworth, you may know how to communicate with spirits, but I know how to create culinary masterpieces that transcend the boundaries of life and death."

With a dramatic flourish, Chef François swept his arm toward the line cooks, his ghostly essence swirling around them. Suddenly, one of the cooks, a lanky young man named Tommy, stiffened as if struck by lightning. His eyes glazed over, and he began to move with a fluid grace that was entirely out of character.

Sabrina watched in astonishment as Tommy, now possessed by Chef François, deftly assembled a tiny, exquisite amuse-bouche on a delicate white plate. The morsel was a perfect balance of colors and textures, a far cry from the usual burger and fries that Tommy would have been preparing.

Oh, for the love of all things supernatural, Sabrina thought, her mind racing with a mix of surprise and frustration. *This is not going to end well.*

As Tommy placed the amuse-bouche on the pass, Chef François relinquished his control, leaving the bewildered line cook staring at his creation in confusion. The ghostly chef turned to Sabrina, a triumphant smile playing on his lips. "You see, ma chère? This is the level of culinary sophistication that the Crossroads Diner deserves."

Sabrina pinched the bridge of her nose, taking a deep breath to calm her fraying nerves. *Okay, Sabrina, think. You've dealt with ghostly meddling before, but never in the form of a culinary coup d'état.*

She glanced at Mort, who had been observing the scene with a mix of amusement and concern. The grim reaper shrugged, as if to say, "Hey, don't look at me. This is your diner, your problem."

Turning back to Chef François, Sabrina forced a smile, her mind working overtime to find a solution that would satisfy both the ghostly chef's ego and maintain the diner's unique charm. "Chef François, I have an idea. What if we..."

Sabrina's mind raced as she tried to formulate a plan that would appease Chef François's culinary ambitions while preserving the diner's beloved atmosphere. "What if we create a special menu section featuring your signature dishes? We can call it 'Chef François's Ethereal Delights' or something equally enticing."

Chef François stroked his ghostly goatee, considering the proposal. "Hmm, a special menu section, you say? That could work, but I insist on having complete creative control over the dishes."

Sabrina nodded, her smile growing more genuine. "Of course, Chef. Your culinary expertise is unparalleled, and we would be honored to showcase your talents."

The ghostly chef's expression softened, his ego sufficiently stroked. "Very well, ma chère. I accept your proposal. I shall begin working on the menu immediately."

As Chef François floated away, already lost in his culinary musings, Sabrina let out a sigh of relief. *Crisis averted, for now,* she thought, exchanging a grateful look with Mort.

However, as she surveyed the diner, taking in the mix of living and ghostly patrons, Sabrina realized that this was only the beginning.

Spectres and Souffles

With the addition of Chef François's ethereal menu, the delicate balance between the two realms would require even more careful management. *It's the price I pay for having a foot in both worlds,* Sabrina mused, a determined glint in her eye. *But I'll be darned if I let it throw my diner off-kilter. I didn't create this paranormal paradise just to have it turn into a spectral circus!*

She straightened her apron, ready to face the challenges ahead. *Time to show these ghosts who's boss,* Sabrina thought with a smirk.

And with that, she strode back into the fray, ready to tackle whatever otherworldly shenanigans came her way.

Chapter 2

The bell above the door chimed, heralding the arrival of a new customer. Sabrina looked up from the coffee pot she was refilling and nearly dropped the carafe. A tall, impeccably dressed man with a curled mustache strode into the Crossroads Diner as if he owned the place. His tailored suit and refined air seemed incongruent with the cozy, retro atmosphere.

Who is this dapper gentleman? Sabrina wondered, taking in his commanding presence. *And what in the world is he doing in my little diner?*

The man made a beeline for the counter, walking with the easy confidence of someone used to being in charge. He came to a stop directly in front of Sabrina and flashed a brilliant smile. "Bonjour, mademoiselle. I am Chef François Dupont, but you may call me 'The Foodie'. I have come to elevate your menu to new heights of culinary excellence!"

Sabrina blinked, taken aback by his bold introduction. "Well, it's a pleasure to meet you François. I'm Sabrina Spellsworth, the owner. Welcome to the Crossroads Diner! What brings you here today?"

"Ah, but of course! I have heard whispers, even from beyond the grave, about your charming little establishment. A place where the living and the dead break bread together - magnifique! But I must confess, your menu...how do you say... lacks a certain je ne sais quoi. Fear not, for I am here to rectify that!" François proclaimed with a flourish of his hand.

Beyond the grave? Oh heavens, he's one of my ghostly patrons! Sabrina realized with a start. She quickly regained her composure and smiled warmly. "That's very kind of you to offer François. Our menu may be simple, but it holds a special place in the hearts, or er, ectoplasms, of our customers. What did you have in mind?"

François leaned forward conspiratorially, his eyes gleaming with excitement. "Picture this - a daring fusion of classic American comfort food and avant-garde French cuisine! Meatloaf Wellington with a truffle demi-glace. Macaroni and cheese soufflé infused with aged Gruyère. Apple pie à la mode...but with a foie gras caramel sauce. The possibilities are endless!"

Sabrina's eyes widened as he rattled off his ideas.

Sabrina cleared her throat, trying to find the right words. "Those dishes sound...intriguing, François. But I'm not sure if they quite fit with the cozy, down-home atmosphere we've cultivated here at the Crossroads Diner."

François waved his hand dismissively. "Nonsense! Your patrons, both living and deceased, deserve to experience the pinnacle of culinary artistry. Imagine their delight when they sink their teeth, or spectral jaws, into a deconstructed s'mores tart with a ghost pepper ganache!"

Ghost pepper ganache? I'm pretty sure that would send even my ghostly customers running for the afterlife! Sabrina thought, struggling to maintain her friendly smile. "I appreciate your enthusiasm, François, but I think we should take things one step at a time. Perhaps we could start with a few small changes and see how our customers respond?"

"Small changes? Pah! Where's your sense of adventure, your passion for pushing boundaries?" François exclaimed, his voice rising with each word. "I tell you, Sabrina, once your customers taste my creations, they will never settle for mere 'comfort food' again!"

Sabrina took a deep breath, her mind racing. *I can't let him completely overhaul the menu, but I don't want to dismiss his ideas outright. There has to be a way to find a balance...*

Sabrina leaned forward, resting her elbows on the counter as she met François's intense gaze. "I hear what you're saying, François, and I don't doubt your culinary prowess. But the Crossroads Diner is more than just a place to eat; it's a haven for those seeking comfort and familiarity, whether they're among the living or the dearly departed."

François scoffed, his eyes narrowing. "Comfort and familiarity? More like stagnation and mediocrity! Your diner has the potential to be a culinary destination, a place where the boundaries between the living and the dead are blurred through the art of gastronomy!"

He just doesn't get it, Sabrina thought, frustration bubbling up inside her. *The Crossroads Diner is special because of its simplicity, not in spite of it.*

"I understand your vision, François," Sabrina said, choosing her words carefully. "But I've built a strong relationship with my customers, and I know they appreciate the diner's charm and the memories it evokes. I'm afraid that if we change too much, too quickly, we might lose that special connection."

François leaned in closer, his voice low and intense. "Sabrina, you're letting your fear of change hold you back. Trust me, I've seen it time and time again. A little ambition goes a long way in this industry. If you don't evolve, you'll be left behind, serving nothing but ghostly gruel and spectral slop."

Sabrina bristled at his words, her jaw clenching. *The nerve of this man! How dare he insult my menu and my customers!*

Taking a calming breath, Sabrina met François's gaze head-on. "I appreciate your perspective, François, but I think we'll have to agree to disagree. The Crossroads Diner is a success because of its unique atmosphere and the connections we've fostered with our customers. I'm not willing to sacrifice that for the sake of culinary trends."

François opened his mouth to respond, but Sabrina held up a hand, silencing him. "However, I'm not opposed to incorporating some of your ideas gradually, as long as they complement our existing menu and don't alienate our regulars. Perhaps we could start with a few daily specials and see how they're received?"

Please, let him meet me halfway, Sabrina thought, hoping to find a compromise that would satisfy both of their visions for the diner.

François's eyes narrowed as he considered Sabrina's proposal. He drummed his fingers on the counter, the rhythmic tapping echoing in the momentary silence between them. "Daily specials," he muttered, his tone laced with a hint of disdain. "I suppose it's a start, but mark my words, Sabrina, once your customers get a taste of my creations, they'll be begging for more."

Sabrina suppressed the urge to roll her eyes. *Confident, isn't he?* she thought wryly. Aloud, she said, "I'm sure they'll appreciate your culinary expertise, François, but let's take it one step at a time. We don't want to overwhelm them with too many changes at once."

François huffed, his shoulders squaring as he drew himself up to his full height. "Fine, we'll do it your way... for now. But don't come crying to me when your customers start demanding more than just meatloaf and apple pie."

As if I would ever come crying to you, Sabrina thought, biting back a retort. Instead, she plastered on a smile and extended her hand. "Then it's settled. We'll introduce a few of your dishes as daily specials and see how it goes from there."

François hesitated for a moment before grasping her hand firmly, his grip a little too tight for Sabrina's liking. "Agreed," he said, his voice low and determined. "But remember, Sabrina, I'm not here to play second fiddle to your comfort food. I'm here to revolutionize this diner, and one way or another, I always get what I want."

With that, he released her hand and turned on his heel, striding towards the kitchen with an air of purpose. Sabrina watched him go, her brow furrowed in concern. *What have I gotten myself into?* she wondered, her mind already racing with the challenges that lay ahead.

As François disappeared into the kitchen, Sabrina let out a long, slow breath, her shoulders sagging as the tension drained from her body. She glanced around the diner, taking in the familiar faces of her regulars, both living and dead. They were the heart and soul of this place, and she'd be damned if she let some fancy chef with an ego the size of Texas change that.

But maybe he's right, a small voice in the back of her mind whispered. *Maybe it's time for a change. Maybe the Crossroads Diner needs a little shaking up.*

Sabrina shook her head, pushing the thought aside. No, she had to trust her instincts. The Crossroads Diner was more than just a restaurant; it was a refuge, a place where the living and the dead could come together in harmony. And she was the one who made that possible.

With a renewed sense of determination, Sabrina straightened her apron and turned to face the counter, ready to take on whatever challenges the day might bring. And if François thought he could just waltz in here and take over, well, he had another thing coming.

I may not be a world-renowned chef, she thought, a small smile tugging at the corners of her lips, *but I know a thing or two about keeping the peace between the living and the dead. And that's a skill that no culinary school can teach.*

As if on cue, the door to the diner swung open, and a group of ghostly construction workers floated in, their translucent bodies shimmering in the sunlight. Sabrina grinned, grabbing a stack of menus and heading over to greet them.

"Welcome to the Crossroads Diner, boys," she said, her voice warm and inviting. "I hope you're ready for some good old-fashioned home cooking, because that's what we're serving up today."

The ghosts chuckled, their laughter echoing through the diner like a gentle breeze. And as Sabrina led them to their usual booth, she couldn't help but feel a sense of pride and belonging. This was her place, her home, and no matter what challenges lay ahead, she knew that she would always find a way to keep the Crossroads Diner a haven for all who entered its doors.

Sabrina returned to the counter, where François was still standing, his arms crossed and a look of skepticism on his face. She took a deep breath, reminding herself to stay calm and composed.

"Look, François," she began, her voice gentle but firm, "I understand that you have a vision for the diner, and I respect that. But you have to understand that this place is more than just a restaurant. It's a sanctuary, a place where the living and the dead can come together and find comfort in each other's company."

François raised an eyebrow, clearly unconvinced. "And you think that serving subpar food is the way to achieve that?" he asked, his tone dripping with condescension.

Sabrina bristled at his words, but refused to let her anger show. Instead, she smiled, her eyes twinkling with a hint of mischief. "I never said anything about serving subpar food," she countered, her voice light and playful. "In fact, I think you'll find that our menu is quite popular with both our living and our deceased customers."

She gestured to the ghostly construction workers, who were happily digging into plates of meatloaf and mashed potatoes, their translucent faces glowing with contentment. "See?" she said, turning back to François with a triumphant grin. "They seem to be enjoying themselves just fine."

Spectres and Souffles

François rolled his eyes, but Sabrina could see a flicker of uncertainty in his expression. *Maybe there's hope for him yet,* she thought, suppressing a smile.

"All right," he said, his voice grudging. "We'll do this your way, for now. But mark my words, Sabrina, once the customers get a taste of my cooking, they'll be begging for more."

Sabrina nodded, her expression serious. "I'm sure they will, François. But for now, let's just focus on finding a way to work together, shall we? After all, we both want what's best for the diner."

François hesitated for a moment, then nodded, his shoulders slumping in defeat. "Fine," he said, his voice gruff. "But don't say I didn't warn you."

With that, he turned and stalked off towards the kitchen, his chef's hat bobbing comically on his head. Sabrina watched him go, a mixture of relief and trepidation swirling in her gut.

Well, she thought, *that went about as well as could be expected.* She knew that the coming weeks would be a challenge, as she and François navigated their differing visions for the diner. But deep down, she had a feeling that everything would work out in the end.

After all, the Crossroads Diner had weathered plenty of storms before, both literal and figurative. And with a little bit of luck, Sabrina knew that they would come out stronger on the other side.

Chapter 3

Sabrina stood frozen in the doorway of the kitchen, her eyes wide with disbelief. The once familiar space buzzed with an otherworldly energy as her ghostly line cooks flitted about, their translucent forms darting from station to station. The air was thick with the aroma of exotic spices and the sizzle of unfamiliar ingredients hitting hot pans.

"What in the name of all things culinary is going on in here?" Sabrina muttered under her breath. She watched as one possessed cook carefully arranged delicate flower petals atop a miniature sculpture made entirely of foie gras. Another piped intricate swirls of beet foam onto a plate already overflowing with garishly colored sauces.

Sabrina's mind raced as she tried to process the scene before her. On one hand, the sheer artistry and skill on display was undeniably impressive. François's culinary genius was clearly influencing her ghostly staff, elevating their creations to heights she had never imagined possible.

But on the other hand, the diner's regulars were expecting their usual comforting fare - fluffy pancakes dripping with syrup, juicy burgers nestled in soft buns, and creamy milkshakes topped with whipped cream. How would they react to being served tiny portions of unpronounceable dishes instead?

As if on cue, a perplexed customer approached the kitchen window, craning his neck to get a better look inside.

"Excuse me, miss," he called out to Sabrina. "I ordered a grilled cheese sandwich twenty minutes ago. Any idea when it might be ready?"

Sabrina plastered on her most charming smile and turned to face the customer. "I apologize for the delay, sir. Our kitchen is just...experimenting with some new techniques at the moment. I'll check on your order right away."

Spectres and Souffles

She spun back around, her smile fading as she surveyed the culinary chaos once more. One line cook was using a blowtorch to caramelize a crust on what appeared to be a deconstructed lemon meringue pie, while another piped delicate dots of caviar onto miniature blini.

Sabrina's brow furrowed as she weighed her options. Confronting François directly could bruise his delicate ghostly ego and risk losing his valuable expertise. But allowing this disruption to continue unchecked could drive away the diner's living clientele and upset the delicate balance she worked so hard to maintain.

Just as she opened her mouth to intervene, a resounding crash echoed through the kitchen.

Sabrina whirled around to find a line cook sprawled on the floor, surrounded by shattered porcelain and a splatter of vibrant green foam. The ghostly chef looked up at her sheepishly, a whisk still clutched in his translucent hand.

"Sorry, boss," he mumbled. "I was trying to perfect my wasabi foam when things got a little out of hand."

Sabrina sighed, her determination to investigate the situation further solidifying with each passing moment. She couldn't let this culinary chaos continue to disrupt the unique atmosphere of her beloved diner.

"Alright, everyone," she announced, clapping her hands together. "Let's take a step back and regroup. I know we're all excited to try new things, but we can't forget what makes the Crossroads Diner special."

The line cooks exchanged guilty glances, their ghostly forms flickering in the fluorescent light. Sabrina softened her tone, her hazel eyes sparkling with understanding.

"I appreciate your enthusiasm, truly. But our customers come here for comfort, familiarity, and a touch of the otherworldly. We need to find a way to balance innovation with tradition."

As the spectral staff nodded in agreement, Sabrina's mind raced with potential solutions. She knew she couldn't tackle this challenge alone – she needed the help of her trusted team of supernatural sleuths.

"Okay, here's the plan," she said, lowering her voice conspiratorially. "I'm going to assemble a crack team of experts to help us navigate this culinary conundrum. In the meantime, let's get back to basics and focus on delivering the classic dishes our customers crave."

The line cooks murmured their assent, their ghostly forms already beginning to drift back to their stations. Sabrina felt a flicker of hope, knowing that with the right approach and a little otherworldly assistance, she could restore harmony to her beloved diner.

But as she turned to head back to the front of the house, a sudden thought stopped her in her tracks. Assembling her team of supernatural sleuths was one thing, but convincing them to take on this unorthodox case might be another matter entirely.

Sabrina squared her shoulders, a determined glint in her eye. She had faced far greater challenges in her time as the proprietor of the Crossroads Diner. With a little charm, a lot of persistence, and maybe a few ghostly favors, she would find a way to bring her team together and solve this culinary mystery once and for all.

As she pushed through the swinging door, Sabrina couldn't help but smile. The Crossroads Diner had always been a place where the living and the dead could come together in harmony – and she would stop at nothing to keep it that way.

But little did she know, an even greater challenge lurked just around the corner, threatening to upend the delicate balance she had worked so hard to maintain...

Sabrina strode into the kitchen, her resolve as solid as the stainless steel countertops. The sight that greeted her was nothing short of surreal. François, the ghostly chef extraordinaire, hovered above a cutting board, his translucent hands deftly arranging a mosaic of vibrant ingredients. The dish was a work of art, a testament to his culinary genius – but it had no place in her diner.

She paused, her breath catching in her throat as she searched for the right words. Confronting a spirit was never easy, especially one with an ego as inflated as François's. But the fate of her beloved diner hung in the balance, and she knew she had to act.

"François," Sabrina called out, her voice steady despite the butterflies in her stomach. "We need to talk."

The spectral chef glanced up, his ethereal eyes narrowing. "Ah, Sabrina, my dear. Come to marvel at my latest creation, have you?"

Spectres and Souffles

Sabrina shook her head, taking a step closer. "No, François. I'm here because we have a problem."

She gestured to the elaborate dish, her brow furrowing. "This... this isn't what the Crossroads Diner is about. We're a place for comfort food, for the dishes that bring people together – both the living and the dead."

François scoffed, his translucent form shimmering with indignation. "Comfort food? Please. My culinary masterpieces are a gift to this establishment. You should be thanking me."

Sabrina's patience wore thin, her determination bubbling to the surface. "I appreciate your passion, François, but you're missing the point. The Crossroads Diner is a place where everyone feels welcome, where they can find a little piece of home. And right now, your 'masterpieces' are driving away the very people we're meant to serve."

The ghostly chef's eyes widened, a flicker of uncertainty crossing his features. Sabrina pressed on, her voice growing stronger with each word.

"I need you to stop possessing my line cooks, François. I need you to understand that this diner is about more than just the food. It's about the people, the memories, the connections we forge across the divide between life and death."

François remained silent, his gaze drifting to the artfully arranged dish before him. Sabrina held her breath, hoping that her words had struck a chord.

But as the seconds ticked by, the tension in the kitchen grew thicker than a roux on a low simmer. François's expression remained inscrutable, his ghostly form as still as a statue.

Sabrina's heart pounded in her chest, the weight of the moment pressing down on her like a ton of bricks. Would François see reason, or would his stubborn pride win out in the end?

The fate of the Crossroads Diner hung in the balance, and Sabrina knew that the next words out of François's mouth could make or break everything she had worked so hard to build...

François's lips curled into a wry smile, his ghostly eyes twinkling with a mixture of amusement and defiance. "Ah, ma chère Sabrina," he purred, his French accent thicker than a freshly made béarnaise sauce. "You speak of memories and connections, but what are those compared to the art of cuisine? The flavors, the textures, the presentation – these are the things that truly matter!"

Sabrina's hands clenched into fists at her sides, her frustration bubbling up like a pot of overheated soup. "François, you're not listening to me!" she exclaimed, her voice echoing off the stainless steel appliances. "This isn't about your ego or your culinary prowess. This is about the heart and soul of the Crossroads Diner!"

The ghostly chef scoffed, waving a dismissive hand in the air. "Heart and soul? Pah! What good are those without the perfect balance of spices, the impeccable plating, the–"

"Enough!" Sabrina slammed her hand down on the counter, sending a shockwave through the kitchen that made even François flinch. "I've tried to be patient, François. I've tried to understand your passion for your craft. But you've crossed a line, and I won't stand for it any longer."

François's eyes narrowed, his ghostly form shimmering with barely contained anger. "You dare to challenge me in my own domain?" he hissed, his voice as cold as a blast chiller.

Sabrina stood her ground, her hazel eyes blazing with determination. "This is my diner, François. My domain. And I will do whatever it takes to protect it, even if that means standing up to a stubborn, egotistical ghost like you!"

The tension in the kitchen reached a boiling point, the air crackling with supernatural energy. François and Sabrina stared each other down, neither willing to back down from their convictions.

But just as it seemed like the confrontation would escalate into a full-blown spectral showdown, a sudden crash from the dining room shattered the moment.

Sabrina whirled around, her heart leaping into her throat. What now? Had François's culinary chaos finally driven her customers to the brink of madness?

She raced out of the kitchen, François hot on her heels, both of them momentarily united by a shared sense of impending doom. But nothing could have prepared them for the sight that awaited them in the dining room...

Spectres and Souffles

As Sabrina burst through the swinging doors, she skidded to a halt, her jaw dropping at the scene before her. The dining room was in utter chaos, with customers ducking for cover as plates of otherworldly food flew through the air, propelled by an unseen force.

"What in the name of all that's holy..." Sabrina muttered, her eyes wide with disbelief.

François, hovering beside her, let out a low whistle. "Now that's what I call a culinary experience!"

Sabrina shot him a withering glare. "This is no time for jokes, François! We have to stop this before someone gets hurt!"

She ducked as a miniature quiche whizzed past her head, narrowly missing her by a hair's breadth. Scanning the room, Sabrina spotted the possessed line cooks, their eyes glazed over as they continued to churn out plate after plate of otherworldly delicacies.

"François, you have to release them from your spell!" Sabrina shouted over the din. "This has gone too far!"

The ghost chef hesitated, his pride warring with the realization that perhaps he had indeed overstepped his bounds. With a heavy sigh, he waved his hand, and the line cooks blinked, stumbling back as the possession lifted.

But the damage had been done. The dining room was a mess, and the customers were in a state of shock. Sabrina knew she had to act fast to salvage the situation.

"Ladies and gentlemen," she called out, her voice steady and reassuring. "I apologize for the unexpected excitement. Please, allow me to offer you a complimentary slice of our famous apple pie as a token of our appreciation for your patience."

The customers, still shaken but mollified by Sabrina's peace offering, began to settle back into their seats. François, chastened, retreated to the kitchen, leaving Sabrina to deal with the aftermath.

As she moved from table to table, offering apologies and slices of pie, Sabrina couldn't help but feel a twinge of sympathy for François. Yes, he had gone too far, but his passion for his craft was undeniable. Perhaps, with a little guidance and a firm hand, she could help him channel that passion in a way that didn't involve possessing her staff and terrorizing her customers.

But for now, Sabrina had a diner to run and a reputation to uphold. She squared her shoulders, plastered on her most winning smile, and set about the task of restoring order to her beloved Crossroads Diner.

Little did she know that this was only the beginning of the otherworldly challenges that lay ahead...

Sabrina marched into the kitchen, her eyes blazing with determination. She found François hunched over a cutting board, meticulously slicing a radish into paper-thin rounds. The possessed line cooks bustled around him, their movements jerky and unnatural.

"François!" Sabrina's voice cut through the chaos. "We need to talk. Now."

The ghostly chef looked up, his translucent brow furrowed. "Mademoiselle Spellsworth, can't you see I'm in the middle of creating a masterpiece?"

"Your 'masterpiece' nearly caused a riot in my diner!" Sabrina planted her hands on her hips, her vintage skirt swishing with the movement. "You can't keep possessing my staff and serving otherworldly dishes to unsuspecting customers."

François scoffed, his ethereal form shimmering with indignation. "You simply don't appreciate the art of haute cuisine."

"I appreciate not having my customers running for the hills!" Sabrina countered, her voice rising. "This is a diner, François, not a Michelin-starred restaurant. People come here for comfort food, not culinary adventures from beyond the grave."

The ghostly chef opened his mouth to argue, but Sabrina held up a hand, silencing him. "No more excuses, François. I need you to stop possessing my line cooks and let them get back to making the dishes that our customers know and love."

François's shoulders slumped, his resistance crumbling under the weight of Sabrina's unwavering resolve. "But... my culinary vision..."

"Can still be realized," Sabrina said, her tone softening. "But in a way that doesn't involve hijacking my staff and terrorizing my customers. We can work together, François, to find a balance between your passion and the needs of the diner."

Spectres and Souffles

The ghostly chef considered her words, his translucent features flickering with a mix of emotions. Finally, he nodded, a reluctant acceptance settling over him. "Very well, Mademoiselle Spellsworth. I will... refrain from my ethereal meddling."

Sabrina smiled, relief washing over her. "Thank you, François. I knew we could find a way to–"

A sudden crash from the dining room interrupted her, followed by a chorus of startled screams. Sabrina's heart leaped into her throat, her mind racing with the possibilities of what fresh otherworldly chaos had descended upon her diner.

She raced out of the kitchen, François close on her heels, only to skid to a halt at the sight that greeted her. There, in the center of the dining room, stood a towering figure made entirely of sausage links, its greasy limbs flailing as it lumbered towards the terrified customers.

"Oh, for the love of..." Sabrina muttered, her eyes widening in disbelief. She glanced back at François, who looked equally stunned. "Please tell me this isn't another one of your culinary creations."

The ghostly chef shook his head, his expression a mix of awe and horror. "I may be passionate, Mademoiselle Spellsworth, but even I have my limits."

Sabrina squared her shoulders, her resolve hardening. It seemed that her work as the proprietor of the Crossroads Diner was far from over. With a ghostly chef by her side and a walking meatball monstrosity on the loose, she knew she had her work cut out for her.

But if there was one thing Sabrina Spellsworth was known for, it was her ability to handle whatever supernatural surprises came her way. And this? This was just another day at the Crossroads Diner.

Sabrina took a deep breath, the adrenaline coursing through her veins as she assessed the situation. The sausage creature had managed to corner a group of terrified customers, its greasy arms reaching out menacingly as it let out a series of guttural grunts.

"François, we need to do something!" Sabrina hissed, her mind racing with potential solutions. She scanned the diner, her eyes landing on the old jukebox in the corner. A sudden idea struck her, and she turned to the ghostly chef with a determined grin.

"Keep that thing distracted," she instructed, already moving towards the jukebox. "I've got a plan."

François nodded, his ethereal form shimmering as he glided towards the sausage creature. With a flourish of his hands, he conjured a barrage of spectral kitchen utensils, sending them flying towards the meaty monstrosity.

As the creature swatted at the ghostly spatulas and whisks, Sabrina reached the jukebox. She quickly flipped through the selection, her fingers hovering over the buttons as she searched for the perfect song.

"Come on, come on," she muttered, her heart pounding in her chest. And then, she found it. With a triumphant grin, she pressed the button, and the opening notes of "Hound Dog" by Elvis Presley filled the diner.

The sausage creature paused, its greasy limbs twitching as the music washed over it. Slowly, it began to sway, its movements becoming more and more rhythmic as the song played on.

Sabrina watched in amazement as the creature's form began to shimmer and shift, the sausage links unraveling and reforming until, in its place, stood a ghostly figure in a leather jacket and a pompadour hairdo.

"Thank you, thank you very much," the figure drawled, its voice a perfect imitation of the King himself. With a final hip shake, the ghost vanished, leaving behind nothing but the faint scent of sausage and a stunned silence.

Sabrina let out a breathless laugh, her heart still racing from the unexpected turn of events. She glanced at François, who looked equally shocked and amused.

"Well, that was certainly a twist," he remarked, a hint of admiration in his voice. "I must say, Mademoiselle Spellsworth, you never cease to amaze me."

Sabrina grinned, the thrill of another supernatural challenge overcome coursing through her veins. "Just another day at the Crossroads Diner," she quipped, already mentally preparing herself for whatever otherworldly surprise might come next.

As Sabrina stepped into the dining room, the lively chatter of her patrons washed over her, a comforting reminder of the unique community she had created within the walls of the Crossroads Diner. The clinking of cutlery against plates and the sizzle of the grill in the kitchen formed a symphony of everyday life, punctuated by the occasional otherworldly whisper or spectral giggle.

She surveyed the room, taking in the eclectic mix of customers - from the elderly ghost couple sharing a milkshake to the werewolf family digging into a platter of rare steaks. Each patron, living or dead, brought their own story and quirks to the table, creating a tapestry of experiences that made the Crossroads Diner truly one-of-a-kind.

As she made her way through the tables, greeting regulars and welcoming new faces, Sabrina couldn't help but feel a sense of pride and purpose. This was her calling, her gift - to provide a haven for those who walked between worlds, to offer comfort and acceptance to all who crossed her threshold.

But with this great responsibility came great challenges, as the recent incident with François and the sausage-link specter had proven. Sabrina knew that her work was far from over, that there would always be new mysteries to unravel and supernatural disturbances to quell.

She glanced over at her team of trusted allies - the mischievous pixie waitress, the sage old ghost who held court at the end of the counter, and the tough-as-nails banshee line cook - and felt a surge of gratitude and determination. Together, they would face whatever the otherworld threw their way, armed with quick wits, endless compassion, and a healthy dose of humor.

Sabrina's thoughts were interrupted by a sudden commotion near the entrance. She turned to see a group of ghosts, their faces etched with worry, rushing towards her.

"Sabrina, you've got to help us!" the leader of the group cried, his spectral form flickering with agitation. "There's a new ghost in town, and he's causing all sorts of trouble. He's scaring the living daylights out of everyone, and we don't know how to stop him!"

She glanced at her team, who were already gathering around her, ready to spring into action.

"Well, then," she said, a grin spreading across her face, "let's go introduce ourselves to this newcomer and show him how we do things at the Crossroads Diner."

Chapter 4

Sabrina paced behind the counter, her vintage heels clicking against the checkerboard floor. She glanced nervously at the kitchen, wincing as a possessed line cook hurled a frying pan across the room with a resounding clang. Another cook, eyes glowing an unnatural green, cackled maniacally while flipping burgers with telekinetic force.

"Oh, for the love of all things holy and deep-fried," Sabrina muttered under her breath. "I'm running a diner, not a supernatural circus!" She ran a hand through her wavy hair, feeling the stress of the escalating situation weighing heavily on her shoulders.

Suddenly, the diner's door swung open with an ominous creak. A tall, gaunt figure glided in, his frame draped in billowing black robes that seemed to absorb the light around him. The temperature in the room plummeted as he approached the counter, his skeletal face partially obscured by the deep hood of his cloak. Sabrina couldn't help but shiver as two glowing pinpricks of light flickered to life in the depths of his eye sockets.

"Well, well, well," the figure spoke, his voice echoing with an otherworldly resonance. "Looks like you've got quite the culinary conundrum on your hands, my dear." He chuckled, the sound sending a chill down Sabrina's spine.

Sabrina straightened her posture, trying to muster an air of confidence. "And you are...?" she asked, raising an eyebrow at the enigmatic intruder.

The figure swept into an exaggerated bow, his robes swirling around him like inky shadows. "Mort Grimshaw, at your service," he announced with a flourish. "Though you may know me by my more... infamous moniker: The Reaper."

Spectres and Souffles

Sabrina's eyes widened as realization dawned on her. A grim reaper? In her diner? She had dealt with her fair share of supernatural entities, but this was a first. "Well, Mr. Grimshaw," she said, trying to keep her voice steady, "I'm not sure what brings you here, but as you can see, I've got my hands full with a bit of a ghostly gourmet situation."

Mort's glowing eye sockets seemed to twinkle with amusement. "Ah, yes. Chef François, I presume?" He turned his gaze towards the kitchen, where the possessed cooks continued their chaotic culinary antics. "I've heard whispers of his... shall we say, spirited return to the culinary world."

Sabrina sighed, leaning against the counter. "You could say that. But I'm at my wit's end trying to figure out how to handle this mess." She looked up at Mort, a glimmer of hope in her eyes. "I don't suppose a grim reaper would be willing to lend a hand in a paranormal culinary crisis?"

Mort let out a dry chuckle, the sound echoing through the diner like a cryptic whisper. "Normally, I wouldn't involve myself in the affairs of the living or the recently deceased," he mused, tapping a bony finger against his chin. "But I must admit, I find myself intrigued by your little predicament here. And, as it so happens, I'm currently on a bit of a sabbatical from my usual soul-reaping duties. A change of pace might be just what the doctor ordered... or, in this case, the grim reaper."

Sabrina couldn't help but smile at Mort's unexpected offer. "I'm not one to look a gift horse in the mouth, especially when that horse is a supernatural entity with an intimate knowledge of the afterlife." She raised an eyebrow, curiosity getting the better of her. "But what makes you so qualified to handle a situation like this?"

Mort's robes rustled as he glided closer to the counter, his imposing frame looming over Sabrina. "My dear, I've been shepherding souls to the great beyond for eons. I've seen every manner of spirit, from the benevolent to the downright malevolent. And in my line of work, you pick up a thing or two about the intricacies of the spirit realm."

He leaned in conspiratorially, his voice dropping to a stage whisper. "Plus, I've got a few tricks up my sleeve that might just come in handy when dealing with a ghost who fancies himself a culinary mastermind."

Sabrina found herself drawn in by Mort's words, her initial hesitation melting away as she considered the wealth of knowledge and experience he possessed. Perhaps having a grim reaper on her side wasn't such a bad idea after all. "Alright, Mr. Grimshaw," she said, a determined glint in her eye. "You've piqued my interest. What do you propose we do about our ghostly chef problem?"

Mort's skeletal grin widened, and he rubbed his bony hands together in anticipation. "Oh, I have a few ideas," he said, his voice laced with dark humor. "But first, let's take a closer look at the kitchen, shall we? I want to see just what kind of mischief our dear Chef François has been cooking up."

With that, Mort glided towards the kitchen, his robes billowing behind him like a cape of shadows. Sabrina took a deep breath, steeling herself for whatever supernatural shenanigans awaited them. As she followed the grim reaper into the culinary chaos, she couldn't help but feel a flutter of excitement in her chest. Perhaps this was the break she needed to finally put an end to the ghostly gourmet's reign of terror.

As they entered the kitchen, Sabrina ducked just in time to avoid a flying spatula, its metal surface gleaming with an otherworldly sheen. The possessed line cooks moved with eerie precision, their eyes glowing an unnatural blue as they chopped, stirred, and sautéed under Chef François's ghostly guidance.

"Ah, the symphony of the kitchen," Mort mused, his eye sockets flickering with amusement. "Though I must say, I prefer the sound of souls crossing the veil to the sizzling of a frying pan."

Sabrina shot him a wry smile, appreciating his ability to find humor in even the most bizarre situations. "Well, I'd rather not have any more souls crossing over in my diner, if it's all the same to you," she quipped, sidestepping a floating whisk that whirred past her head.

Mort chuckled, a sound that echoed through the kitchen like the tolling of a distant bell. "Fair enough," he conceded, his gaze scanning the organized chaos before them. "Now, let's talk about the afterlife, shall we?"

Sabrina nodded, her curiosity piqued. She had always wondered about the intricacies of the spirit world, and who better to learn from than a grim reaper himself?

"You see," Mort began, his voice taking on a professorial tone, "there are many planes of existence beyond the mortal realm. Some spirits linger in the space between, unable to move on due to unfinished business or a strong emotional attachment to the physical world."

Sabrina listened intently, her mind racing with questions. "So, ghosts like Chef François, they're stuck here because of their ties to the living world?" she asked, her brow furrowed in concentration.

"Precisely," Mort confirmed, nodding his hooded head. "But it's not just ghosts you'll encounter. There are poltergeists, specters, and even the occasional wraith, each with their own unique characteristics and abilities."

Sabrina's eyes widened, a mixture of fascination and trepidation swirling within her. "And how do we deal with them?" she inquired, her voice barely audible above the clanging of pots and pans.

Mort's skeletal fingers tapped against the handle of his scythe, a contemplative gesture that seemed almost human. "It depends on the spirit," he explained, his voice low and measured. "Some can be reasoned with, while others may require a more... forceful approach."

Sabrina swallowed hard, the weight of her newfound knowledge settling upon her shoulders like a ghostly mantle. She opened her mouth to ask another question, but her words were cut short by a sudden, earsplitting crash from the other side of the kitchen.

Chef François's ghostly form hovered above the stove, his translucent face contorted in rage. "You dare to interfere with my culinary masterpiece?" he bellowed, his voice reverberating through the kitchen like a clap of thunder. "I will not allow it!"

With a wave of his spectral hand, the possessed line cooks turned to face Sabrina and Mort, their eyes blazing with an unholy light. They advanced slowly, their movements jerky and unnatural, like puppets on invisible strings.

Sabrina's heart raced, her palms slick with sweat as she glanced at Mort, desperate for guidance. The grim reaper remained impassive, his eye sockets fixed upon the approaching horde of culinary zombies.

"Well," he drawled, his voice dripping with irony, "it seems our ghostly chef has a bone to pick with us. How delightfully macabre."

As the possessed cooks drew closer, their hands outstretched like claws, Sabrina couldn't help but wonder if Mort's dark humor would be enough to save them from the wrath of a spectral sous chef scorned.

Mort stepped forward, placing himself between Sabrina and the advancing line cooks. His skeletal hand reached into the folds of his black robes, and he withdrew a gleaming silver scythe, its blade shimmering with an otherworldly light.

"Now, now," he chided, his voice a silken purr, "let's not get too carried away, shall we? After all, we're all friends here in the afterlife."

Sabrina watched in awe as Mort twirled the scythe with a casual grace, the weapon seeming to dance in his bony grasp. The possessed cooks hesitated, their glazed eyes flickering with uncertainty.

"Chef François," Mort called out, his gaze fixed upon the ghostly figure hovering above the stove, "I understand your passion for the culinary arts, but this is hardly the way to go about it. Why don't we sit down and have a little chat, spirit to spirit?"

The ghostly chef's face twisted with rage, his translucent form shimmering like a heat haze. "You dare to lecture me, Reaper?" he spat, his voice dripping with contempt. "I am the master of this kitchen, and I will not be denied my rightful place!"

Mort sighed, his shoulders slumping in a gesture of mock defeat. "Very well, if you insist on being difficult..." He turned to Sabrina, his eye sockets glinting with mischief. "My dear, I do apologize for the mess this is about to make."

With a flick of his wrist, Mort sent the scythe spinning through the air, its blade slicing through the ghostly chef's form like a hot knife through butter. Chef François let out a howl of rage, his spectral body dissipating like smoke in the wind.

The possessed line cooks collapsed like marionettes with their strings cut, their bodies crumpling to the floor in a tangle of limbs. Sabrina rushed forward, her heart in her throat, but a quick check revealed that they were merely unconscious, their chests rising and falling with steady breaths.

"Mort," Sabrina whispered, her voice trembling with a mixture of awe and relief, "I can't thank you enough. I don't know what I would have done without your help."

The grim reaper shrugged, a hint of a smile playing at the corners of his skeletal mouth. "Think nothing of it, my dear. It's all in a day's work for a reaper on sabbatical."

Sabrina couldn't help but laugh, the tension draining from her body in a rush of giddy relief. "I never thought I'd say this, but I'm glad to have a grim reaper on my side."

Mort chuckled, his eye sockets glinting with amusement. "And I never thought I'd find myself playing ghostbuster in a haunted diner, but life (or rather, death) is full of surprises."

As they surveyed the aftermath of the ghostly confrontation, Sabrina felt a renewed sense of determination filling her heart. With Mort by her side, she knew that they would get to the bottom of this culinary mystery, one way or another.

But even as the thought crossed her mind, a sudden, chilling realization sent a shiver down her spine. Chef François's ghost may have been temporarily dispersed, but she had a sinking feeling that this was only the beginning of their otherworldly troubles.

Sabrina and Mort huddled together at a corner booth, their heads bent low as they discussed their next steps. The diner's neon lights cast an eerie glow across their faces, highlighting the determination in Sabrina's eyes and the mischievous glint in Mort's eye sockets.

"So, what's our plan of attack?" Sabrina asked, absently twirling a strand of her hair around her finger. "We can't just sit around and wait for Chef François to possess more of my staff."

Mort leaned back, his bony fingers steepled beneath his chin. "Well, we could always try a good old-fashioned exorcism. I know a guy who knows a guy..."

Sabrina raised an eyebrow, a smirk tugging at the corner of her mouth. "An exorcism? In my diner? I don't think so. I'd like to keep my customers, both living and dead, thank you very much."

"Fair enough," Mort conceded, his shoulders shaking with a silent chuckle. "I suppose we could try reaching out to the spirit realm directly. See if we can get some answers straight from the source."

Sabrina's eyes widened, a mix of excitement and trepidation coursing through her veins. "You mean like a séance? I've never done anything like that before."

Mort waved a dismissive hand. "It's not as complicated as it sounds. All we need is a few candles, some incense, and a healthy dose of otherworldly mojo. Lucky for you, I've got plenty of that to spare."

Sabrina bit her lip, weighing the options in her mind. On one hand, the idea of communicating with the dead sent a thrill of anticipation down her spine. On the other hand, she couldn't shake the feeling that they were treading on dangerous ground.

"I don't know, Mort," she said, her voice hesitant. "What if we accidentally summon something worse than Chef François?"

The grim reaper leaned forward, his eye sockets glowing with an intensity that made Sabrina's breath catch in her throat. "Sabrina, my dear, I've been guiding souls to the afterlife for eons. There's not much out there that can rattle these old bones. Trust me, we'll be fine."

Sabrina took a deep breath, the knot of tension in her chest loosening slightly at Mort's reassuring words. "Okay," she said, a smile spreading across her face. "Let's do it. Let's have a séance."

Mort clapped his hands together, a wicked grin stretching across his skeletal face. "Excellent! I'll gather the necessary supplies. You just make sure the diner is cleared out and ready for some supernatural shenanigans."

As they rose from the booth, Sabrina couldn't help but feel a sense of exhilaration coursing through her veins. She was about to embark on a journey into the unknown, and with Mort by her side, she felt like anything was possible.

But even as they set about their preparations, Sabrina couldn't shake the nagging feeling that they were about to unleash something far more sinister than they ever could have imagined. The shadows seemed to lengthen around her, and the air crackled with an unseen energy that sent shivers down her spine.

What dark secrets lay hidden in the spirit realm, waiting to be uncovered? And more importantly, would they be ready to face them when the time came.

As the last of the patrons filed out of the diner, Sabrina locked the door and turned to face Mort. "Alright, let's get this séance started." She

Spectres and Souffles

rubbed her hands together, a mixture of nervousness and excitement coursing through her veins.

Mort nodded, his skeletal grin unwavering. "I've got everything we need right here." He patted the ancient-looking leather satchel slung over his shoulder. "Let's head to the kitchen. It's the heart of the diner, and I have a feeling that's where we'll find the answers we seek."

Sabrina led the way, her vintage heels clicking against the checkered floor. As they entered the kitchen, the usually bustling space seemed eerily quiet, the only sound being the hum of the refrigerator. Mort cleared a space on the center prep table and began laying out an assortment of candles, herbs, and strange-looking artifacts.

"Are you sure you know what you're doing?" Sabrina asked, eyeing the peculiar items skeptically.

Mort chuckled, the sound echoing hollowly in the empty kitchen. "I've been doing this for centuries, my dear. Trust me, I'm a professional."

Sabrina watched as Mort meticulously arranged the candles in a circle, his bony fingers moving with surprising dexterity. He then sprinkled a mixture of herbs in the center and began chanting in a language Sabrina couldn't understand.

As the chanting grew louder, the candles flickered to life, casting an eerie glow across the kitchen. Sabrina felt a chill run down her spine, and the hair on the back of her neck stood on end. Suddenly, a gust of icy wind swept through the room, extinguishing the candles and plunging them into darkness.

"Mort?" Sabrina called out, her voice trembling slightly. "What's happening?"

But before Mort could respond, a sinister laugh echoed through the kitchen, sending shivers down Sabrina's spine. She spun around, her eyes straining to see in the darkness, but she could make out nothing more than shadowy figures darting about the room.

"Sabrina Spellsworth," a voice hissed, seeming to come from everywhere and nowhere at once. "You dare to summon us? You have no idea what you've unleashed."

Sabrina's heart raced as she realized the gravity of their situation. They had indeed unleashed something, and now they would have to face the consequences head-on. She glanced at Mort, his glowing eye sockets the only source of light in the darkness, and knew that together, they would have to fight whatever malevolent force they had awakened.

The darkness engulfed the kitchen, broken only by the eerie glow of Mort's eye sockets. Sabrina's heart pounded as she strained to see through the inky blackness, her senses on high alert.

"Show yourself!" Sabrina demanded, her voice wavering slightly as she tried to project confidence. "We're not afraid of you!"

Mort chuckled darkly beside her. "Speak for yourself, doll. I've seen things that would make even the bravest souls quake in their boots."

A gust of frigid air whipped through the room, sending pots and pans clattering to the floor. Sabrina flinched, instinctively grabbing Mort's bony arm for support. The sinister laughter grew louder, echoing off the walls and seeming to come from every direction at once.

"Foolish mortals," the voice sneered. "You have no power here. This is my domain now."

Sabrina's mind raced, trying to formulate a plan. She knew they needed to act fast before things escalated further. Suddenly, an idea struck her.

"Mort, the sage!" she hissed urgently. "We need to cleanse the space!"

Mort nodded, his skeletal hand already reaching into the depths of his robes. "Way ahead of you, boss."

With a flourish, he produced a bundle of dried sage and a lighter. Sabrina snatched them from his grasp and quickly set the sage ablaze. The pungent aroma filled the air as she waved the smoldering bundle, sending tendrils of smoke curling through the darkness.

"By the power of sage and light, I banish you from this site!" Sabrina chanted, her voice growing stronger with each word.

The laughter faltered, replaced by an angry hiss. The shadows seemed to writhe and twist, fighting against the cleansing smoke. Sabrina and Mort stood back to back, the sage held aloft like a beacon in the darkness.

Suddenly, a gust of wind surged through the kitchen, slamming the doors shut and rattling the windows. The laughter grew to a deafening crescendo, and Sabrina felt an icy hand close around her throat, squeezing the air from her lungs.

Spectres and Souffles

She gasped, struggling against the invisible grip, but it only tightened its hold. Spots danced before her eyes as her vision began to blur. Beside her, Mort let out a string of colorful curses, his scythe slashing through the air in a futile attempt to fend off their unseen attacker.

Just as Sabrina felt her consciousness slipping away, the pressure around her neck suddenly vanished. She collapsed to the floor, gulping in lungfuls of air as Mort knelt beside her, his bony hand resting reassuringly on her shoulder.

"Well, that was a close one," he quipped, his voice strained with concern. "You okay, boss?"

Sabrina nodded, rubbing her bruised throat. "I'll live. But what the hell was that thing?"

Mort shook his head, his eye sockets glowing with a newfound intensity. "I don't know, but whatever it is, it's not playing around. We're going to need backup if we want to take this thing down."

Sabrina pushed herself to her feet. "Then let's get to work. We've got a kitchen to reclaim and a ghost to bust."

Chapter 5

Sabrina burst through the swinging kitchen doors, Mort gliding eerily behind her. The clanging pots and sizzling pans did little to mask the otherworldly chaos that had taken over her beloved diner. Her eyes narrowed as she spotted François, the ghostly chef, flitting about the kitchen with a mischievous grin on his translucent face.

"François!" Sabrina called out, her voice a mix of exasperation and determination. "We need to talk. Now."

The spectral chef paused mid-stir, his ladle still dripping with an iridescent, glowing sauce. He turned to face Sabrina and Mort, his expression one of feigned innocence. "Ah, ma chère Sabrina! And Monsieur Grimshaw, what a pleasant surprise. To what do I owe this unexpected visit?"

Mort's eye sockets flickered with an eerie blue light as he spoke, his voice echoing with the weight of centuries. "Cut the pleasantries, François. We know you're behind all this supernatural mayhem in the diner."

François waved his hand dismissively, sending a shower of spectral spices cascading through the air. "Moi? I am but a humble chef, dedicated to creating culinary delights for our esteemed patrons, both living and dead."

The nerve of this guy, Sabrina thought, her patience wearing thin. *How am I supposed to run a diner when he's turning the kitchen into his own personal playground?*

She stepped forward, her vintage dress swishing around her ankles as she fixed François with a stern gaze. "Listen, François, I appreciate your enthusiasm, but you're causing more trouble than a poltergeist at a china shop. We need to find a way to work together, not against each other."

François's smug smile only grew wider. "Ah, but where is the fun in that, ma chère? A little chaos adds spice to the afterlife, non?" He chuckled, the sound echoing eerily off the stainless steel surfaces.

Mort's grip tightened on his scythe, the ancient weapon glinting menacingly in the fluorescent light. "Fun's over, chef. Time to hang up your apron and let Sabrina run her diner in peace."

The ghostly chef's eyes narrowed, a dangerous glint lurking within their spectral depths. "You dare to challenge me in my own kitchen? Very well, let us see who truly holds the power here." With a flick of his wrist, François sent a barrage of ghostly utensils flying towards Sabrina and Mort, the air crackling with otherworldly energy.

Sabrina ducked, her heart racing as a spectral spatula whizzed past her ear. *This is getting out of hand*, she thought, her mind racing to find a solution. *We need to find a way to stop François before he turns my diner into a full-blown supernatural battlefield!*

As Sabrina and Mort dodged the onslaught of ghostly kitchenware, François's laughter filled the air, a discordant melody of mischief and mayhem. With a theatrical wave of his hand, the spectral chef conjured a swirling vortex of ethereal ingredients, their otherworldly hues casting an eerie glow throughout the kitchen.

"Behold, my culinary creations!" François declared, his voice dripping with wicked delight. From the depths of the ghostly maelstrom, a legion of spectral appetizers emerged, their forms twisted and grotesque. Translucent shrimp cocktails scuttled across the counters, their beady eyes glowing with malevolent intent. Ghostly meatballs floated through the air, leaving trails of ectoplasmic residue in their wake.

Sabrina's eyes widened in shock as a phantasmal slider soared towards her face, its spectral bun snapping menacingly. She swatted it away with a nearby frying pan, sending it splattering against the wall in a burst of ghostly condiments. "Mort!" she called out, her voice tinged with panic. "We need to find a way to stop these things before they wreak havoc on the diner!"

Mort swung his scythe in a wide arc, cleaving a dozen ghostly canapés in half. The severed appetizers flopped to the ground, their movements erratic and unsettling. "I'm open to suggestions, boss," he grunted, his skeletal face contorted in concentration as he fended off a barrage of possessed crostini.

François cackled with glee, reveling in the chaos he had unleashed. "Surrender to the superior culinary prowess of François, the greatest chef in the afterlife!" He twirled his spectral mustache, his eyes alight with manic joy.

Sabrina gritted her teeth, her determination rising above the fear that gripped her heart. She refused to let her beloved diner fall victim to François's twisted games. As she batted away a ghostly spring roll with a baking sheet, her mind raced to find a way to turn the tables on the malevolent chef. *There has to be a way to beat him at his own game*, she thought, her brow furrowed in concentration. *But how do you outsmart a ghost with an ego the size of the astral plane?*

Mort's scythe sliced through a spectral quiche, sending bits of ectoplasmic filling splattering across the kitchen. "Sabrina, we need to find the source of his power," he called out, his voice echoing with an otherworldly timbre. "Every ghost has an anchor to the living world. If we can identify and neutralize it, we might be able to stop this culinary catastrophe!"

Sabrina nodded, her hazel eyes scanning the kitchen for any clues. Suddenly, her gaze landed on the gleaming set of antique knives hanging on the wall behind François. The blades seemed to pulse with an eerie, greenish light, and she could have sworn she saw wisps of spectral energy emanating from their handles.

"The knives!" she exclaimed, pointing towards the collection with a trembling finger. "I think they might be the key to his power. We need to separate him from them somehow."

Mort followed her gaze, his skeletal grin widening as he caught on to her plan. "Clever girl," he chuckled, his eye sockets glowing with newfound determination. "I'll keep these ghostly hors d'oeuvres at bay while you figure out how to get those knives away from him."

Sabrina took a deep breath, steeling herself for the task ahead. She knew she had to be quick and decisive if she wanted to put an end to François's reign of terror. With a nod to Mort, she grabbed a nearby rolling pin and charged towards the ghostly chef, her vintage dress swishing around her legs as she moved.

Spectres and Souffles

This ends now, François, she thought, her jaw set with resolve. *You've messed with the wrong diner owner, and I'm about to show you what happens when you cross Sabrina Spellsworth!*

As she neared the spectral chef, François spun around, his translucent form shimmering with malevolent energy. "Foolish mortal!" he sneered, brandishing a ghostly cleaver. "You dare to challenge the master of paranormal cuisine? Prepare to be diced, julienned, and served as a side dish to my glorious creations!"

The clash of metal against metal rang out through the kitchen as Sabrina's rolling pin met François's cleaver in a shower of sparks. The battle for the soul of the diner had begun, and the fate of both the living and the dead hung in the balance.

Sabrina ducked and weaved, her reflexes honed by years of dodging ghostly diners and their otherworldly demands. François's cleaver sliced through the air, narrowly missing her as she danced around the kitchen, her heart pounding in her chest.

"Mort!" she called out, her voice strained with exertion. "How are you holding up over there?"

The reaper grunted, his scythe a blur of motion as he fended off a barrage of spectral shrimp cocktails. "Oh, you know," he quipped, his skeletal grin never wavering, "just another day in the afterlife. Remind me to add 'ghostly appetizer wrangler' to my resume."

Despite the gravity of the situation, Sabrina couldn't help but chuckle. Leave it to Mort to find humor in the midst of a supernatural battle royale. She turned her attention back to François, her eyes narrowing as she sought an opening in his defenses.

There! she thought, spotting a momentary gap in the ghostly chef's guard. With a swift motion, she lunged forward, her rolling pin poised to strike. But François was too quick, his cleaver slicing through the air and knocking the makeshift weapon from her grasp.

Sabrina stumbled back, her eyes wide with surprise. *This is bad,* she realized, her mind racing as she sought a way out of her predicament. *If I can't get those knives away from him, we'll be trapped in this kitchen forever, haunted by an endless parade of paranormal hors d'oeuvres.*

As if sensing her desperation, the spectral creations redoubled their efforts, surging forward in a tidal wave of ghostly canapés and eerie entrées. Mort found himself overwhelmed, his scythe barely able to keep the horde at bay.

"Sabrina!" he cried out, his voice tinged with uncharacteristic worry. "I don't know how much longer I can hold them off. We need a new plan, and fast!"

Sabrina's mind raced, her gaze darting around the kitchen in search of inspiration. T*hink, Sabrina, think!* she chided herself, her heart pounding in her ears. *There has to be a way to stop François and his culinary creations before they consume us all.* Suddenly, her eyes fell upon the walk-in freezer, its stainless steel door gleaming in the fluorescent light. A wild, desperate idea began to take shape in her mind, a plan so crazy it just might work.

"Mort!" she shouted, her voice ringing with newfound determination. "I need you to trust me. When I give the signal, I want you to lure François and his appetizers towards the freezer. Can you do that?"

The reaper paused, his eye sockets glowing with curiosity. "I'm not sure where you're going with this, Sabrina, but I'm game. Just say the word, and I'll have these ghostly gourmands eating out of the palm of my hand... figuratively speaking, of course."

Sabrina nodded, a fierce grin spreading across her face. *Hold on tight, François,* she thought, her spirit soaring with renewed hope. *You're about to learn what happens when you mess with a Spellsworth and her trusty reaper sidekick. It's time to put this culinary nightmare on ice, once and for all!*

Mort sprang into action, his scythe slicing through the air as he herded the spectral appetizers towards the freezer. "Come on, you bite-sized menaces!" he taunted, his voice dripping with sarcasm. "Let's see if you can handle a little cold shoulder!"

François watched in disbelief as his creations were corralled by the reaper, their ghostly forms shimmering with confusion. "What are you doing, you meddlesome mort?" he sputtered, his translucent face contorted with rage. "You cannot hope to defeat me with mere refrigeration!"

Sabrina smirked, her eyes sparkling with mischief. "Oh, but I can, François. You see, I've just remembered a little secret about ghostly gastronomy." She reached for the freezer door, her fingers tingling with anticipation. "Spirits may not feel the cold, but their manifestations sure do. And when it comes to spectral sustenance, there's nothing quite like a deep freeze to send them packing!"

With a triumphant cry, Sabrina flung open the freezer door, unleashing a blast of icy air that engulfed the kitchen. The spectral appetizers let out a collective shriek as the cold seeped into their ethereal forms, their movements growing sluggish and stilted.

Mort seized the opportunity, his scythe flashing as he herded the weakened spirits into the freezer's depths. "Time to chill out, my little paranormal puffs!" he quipped, his eye sockets blazing with dark delight. "Looks like your culinary reign of terror has come to a frosty end."

As the last of the appetizers vanished into the freezer, Sabrina slammed the door shut, a sigh of relief escaping her lips. The kitchen was still, the only sound the gentle hum of the appliances and the distant chatter of oblivious diners.

François stood in shocked silence, his ghostly form flickering with impotent rage. "This isn't over, Spellsworth," he hissed, his voice a venomous whisper. "I will have my revenge, and your precious diner will be mine!"

Sabrina merely smiled, her eyes alight with confidence. "Bring it on, François. As long as I have Mort by my side and a fully stocked freezer, you don't stand a ghost of a chance."

With a final, frustrated howl, François vanished, leaving Sabrina and Mort alone in the kitchen. The reaper turned to her, his skeletal grin a touch wider than usual. "Well, that was certainly a chilling climax," he remarked, his voice tinged with admiration. "Remind me never to get on your bad side, especially when there's a walk-in freezer nearby."

Sabrina laughed, the tension of the battle melting away. "Oh, Mort," she said, her tone warm with affection. "You know I'd never put you on ice. After all, what would I do without my favorite partner in paranormal crime-solving?"

The reaper chuckled, his eye sockets softening with a hint of fondness. "I suppose you're right, Sabrina. We make quite the team, don't we? The ghost-seeing diner owner and the sarcastic reaper, ready to take on whatever supernatural shenanigans come our way."

As they shared a moment of camaraderie, Sabrina couldn't help but feel a sense of triumph. They had faced François's spectral onslaught and emerged victorious, their bond stronger than ever. *But,* she thought, a flicker of unease creeping into her mind, *this is far from over. With François still lurking in the shadows, who knows what ghostly challenges await us in the days to come?*

Sabrina's brow furrowed as she surveyed the aftermath of their battle. Spectral remnants of François's culinary creations littered the kitchen floor, slowly dissipating into wispy tendrils. She sighed, her mind already racing with the implications of their ghostly adversary's newfound power.

"We can't let him continue like this," she declared, her voice filled with determination. "If François keeps unleashing his spectral appetizers on unsuspecting patrons, it's only a matter of time before someone gets hurt... or worse."

Mort nodded, his scythe gleaming as he leaned against the stainless steel counter. "Agreed. But how do we stop a ghost with a penchant for paranormal cuisine? It's not like we can just slap a 'No Haunting' sign on the door and call it a day."

Sabrina paced the kitchen, her vintage heels clicking against the tile. She absently tucked a stray lock of hair behind her ear, her mind whirring with possibilities. Suddenly, her eyes widened, and a slow grin spread across her face.

"I've got it!" she exclaimed, whirling to face Mort. "What if we fight fire with fire... or in this case, ghost with ghost?"

The reaper tilted his head, intrigue glinting in his eye sockets. "Go on..."

"We need to find a spirit who can match François's culinary prowess," Sabrina explained, her words tumbling out in an excited rush. "Someone who can create ethereal dishes that will counteract his malevolent munchies. And I think I know just the ghost for the job."

Mort's grin widened, his teeth gleaming in the fluorescent light. "Sabrina, you're a genius. A mad, brilliant genius. I knew there was a reason I stuck around this diner, besides the unlimited supply of spectral snacks."

Sabrina laughed, the sound ringing through the kitchen like a bell. "Well, what can I say? When you've been serving the supernatural for as long as I have, you learn a thing or two about ghostly gastronomy."

Spectres and Souffles

As they set about cleaning up the kitchen, Sabrina's mind raced with the details of their plan. She knew it wouldn't be easy, but with Mort by her side and a spectral chef on their team, they just might have a chance at stopping François's reign of terror.

But first, she thought, a wry smile tugging at her lips, *we need to find our ghostly gourmet. And something tells me that's going to be an adventure in itself.*

As the sun dipped below the horizon, Sabrina and Mort made their way through the bustling streets of the city. The air was thick with the aroma of sizzling food and the chatter of passersby, but the duo remained focused on their mission, their steps purposeful and determined.

"So, where exactly are we headed?" Mort asked, his voice barely audible over the din of the crowd.

Sabrina glanced at him, a mischievous twinkle in her eye. "To the one place where you can find the most talented, the most passionate, and the most eccentric chefs in the city: the Culinary Institute of Ethereal Arts."

Mort's jaw dropped, his eyes widening in surprise. "The Culinary Institute of Ethereal Arts? You mean the place where the greatest ghostly chefs of all time go to hone their skills and create culinary masterpieces?"

Sabrina nodded, a grin spreading across her face. "The very same. And if we're going to find a spirit who can match François's skill and creativity, that's where we need to start."

As they approached the institute, a grand, gothic building with towering spires and intricate carvings, Sabrina felt a thrill of excitement run through her.

But as they stepped through the ornate double doors, Sabrina and Mort were greeted by a sight that made their blood run cold. The once-bustling halls of the institute were empty, the classrooms and kitchens eerily silent. It was as if all the ghostly chefs had vanished into thin air.

"What happened here?" Mort whispered, his voice echoing in the deserted corridors.

Sabrina shook her head, a sense of unease settling in the pit of her stomach. "I don't know, but something tells me it has something to do with François."

As they ventured deeper into the institute, their footsteps echoing on the polished marble floors, Sabrina and Mort couldn't shake the feeling that they were being watched. The shadows seemed to flicker and dance, as if hiding secrets within their depths.

Suddenly, a voice rang out, shattering the silence like a gunshot. "Well, well, well. Look who decided to pay us a visit."

Sabrina and Mort whirled around, their hearts pounding in their chests. There, standing before them, was a figure cloaked in darkness, a sinister smile playing on their lips.

"Who are you?" Sabrina demanded, her voice trembling slightly.

The figure stepped forward, the light from the flickering candles casting an eerie glow on their face. "I'm the one who's going to make sure you never interfere with François's plans again."

And with that, the figure lunged forward, a weapon glinting in their hand, ready to strike.

Chapter 6

The bell above the door jangled violently as Sabrina slammed a stack of case files onto the counter. "We're in over our heads, Mort. This celebrity chef murder is more tangled than a plate of angel hair pasta."

Mort glanced up from polishing his scythe, his skeletal grin somehow conveying amusement. "Well, I could always pay the killer a personal visit and sort things out the old-fashioned way."

Sabrina shot him a withering look. "Tempting, but let's call that Plan B. What we need are reinforcements - fresh eyes and unique skills to help crack this supernatural spaghetti bowl."

As if on cue, the diner's door burst open with a gust of wind and a crackle of energy. In swept a vibrant whirlwind of red hair, black leather, and jingling bracelets. Sabrina blinked as the newcomer struck a dramatic pose, surrounded by the faint scent of cinnamon and smoke.

"Did someone say unique skills?" the woman asked with a mischievous grin. "Pepper Thornfield, explosive witch extraordinaire, at your service!"

Mort leaned towards Sabrina, his voice a dry whisper. "I think your fresh eyes just walked in, and they're looking rather...spicy."

Sabrina appraised Pepper, taking in her eclectic mix of flowy skirts, biker boots, and rune-inscribed leather jacket. She had to admit, the witch radiated a magnetic charm, her emerald eyes sparkling with barely contained mischief.

"Welcome to the Crossroads Diner, Pepper," Sabrina greeted warmly. "I'm Sabrina, and this is my partner, Mort. We could definitely use a witch with your talents."

Pepper sauntered over to the counter, her bangles clinking musically. "Well, you're in luck! My spells pack a punch...though I can't always guarantee what kind. Last week, I tried to summon a hellhound and ended up with a pack of flaming Chihuahuas instead."

Mort chuckled darkly. "Sounds like my kind of party."

Pepper's unpredictable magic could be just the wild card they needed to unravel this mystery. She felt a flicker of hope amidst the frustration of dead ends and cold leads.

"Pull up a stool, Pepper," Sabrina invited, pushing a mug of steaming coffee towards the witch. "We've got a supernatural knot to untangle, and something tells me you're just the woman to help us do it."

As Pepper plopped onto the stool, crackling with barely-contained magical energy, Sabrina couldn't help but feel the tides turning in their favor. With a grim reaper, a spell-slinging witch, and a haunted diner at her disposal, the ghostly killer cowered somewhere in the shadows, yet fate undoubtedly plotted their reckoning this very moment.

Pepper leaned forward. "Supernatural knot, you say? I'm all ears, darling. Lay it on me."

Sabrina took a deep breath. "We're investigating a murder, Pepper. A celebrity chef was found dead in our kitchen, and we suspect there's a ghostly killer on the loose."

Mort nodded solemnly, his skeletal fingers wrapped around his own mug of coffee. "And not just any celebrity chef. François Fromage was the big cheese in the culinary world. His death has left a lot of people feeling bleu."

Pepper snorted, nearly choking on her coffee. "Leave it to the Grim Reaper to make a pun at a time like this."

Sabrina pressed on, her voice earnest. "Pepper, your unique abilities could be the key to cracking this case wide open. We need someone who can think outside the box, someone who isn't afraid to take risks."

Pepper's brow furrowed, a flicker of doubt crossing her features. "I don't know, Sabrina. My spells are about as predictable as a drunken unicorn in a china shop. What if I make things worse?"

Mort leaned forward, his voice uncharacteristically gentle. "Kid, I've been around the block a few times, and I know potential when I see it. Your magic may be chaotic, but it's also powerful. Embrace it."

Spectres and Souffles

Sabrina reached out, placing a reassuring hand on Pepper's arm. "We believe in you, Pepper. This is your chance to prove yourself, to show the world what you're truly capable of."

Pepper's eyes darted between Sabrina and Mort, a war of emotions playing out on her face. The desire to make a difference, to live up to her family's legacy, battled against the fear of her own unpredictable powers.

Sabrina's heart raced as she watched Pepper, silently willing her to take the leap of faith. She knew, deep down, that Pepper was the missing piece to their supernatural puzzle.

After what felt like an eternity, Pepper's shoulders straightened, a determined glint in her eye. "Alright, I'm in. Let's catch ourselves a ghostly killer and show them what happens when they mess with us."

Sabrina grinned, a wave of relief washing over her. As the unlikely trio huddled together, plotting their next move, the air crackled with magical energy.

The ghostly killer may have thought they had the upper hand, but they had no idea what they were up against. A grim reaper with a penchant for puns, a witch with explosive potential, and a diner owner with a heart of gold - together, they were an unstoppable force.

As the sun dipped below the horizon, casting an eerie glow through the diner's windows, Sabrina couldn't shake the feeling that this was just the beginning of a wild and unpredictable ride.

Just as Sabrina, Mort, and Pepper were about to dive into their plan of action, a soft whimper caught their attention. Sabrina's eyes widened as she spotted a translucent, scruffy little dog cautiously padding towards them, his tail tucked between his legs.

"Well, hello there, little fella," Sabrina cooed, crouching down to get a better look at the ghostly canine. "Where did you come from?"

The dog, sensing Sabrina's warmth, hesitantly approached her, his ethereal nose twitching as he sniffed her outstretched hand. Sabrina couldn't help but smile at the sight of his soulful eyes and tousled fur, which seemed to shimmer in the diner's soft light.

Mort tilted his head, studying the spectral pup. "I've seen this little guy around the diner before, always watching from a distance. Never thought he'd muster up the courage to come say hello."

Pepper, her curiosity piqued, knelt beside Sabrina. "He seems so timid, like he's been through a lot. Poor little guy."

As if understanding their words, the ghost dog let out a soft bark, his tail wagging tentatively. Sabrina gently scratched behind his ears, marveling at the strange sensation of her fingers passing through his translucent form.

"I think he likes you," Mort chuckled, watching as the dog leaned into Sabrina's touch.

She had always believed that every spirit had a purpose, and the sudden appearance of this gentle soul couldn't be a mere coincidence. "You know, I have a feeling this little guy might be just what we need to crack this case wide open."

Pepper raised an eyebrow, intrigued. "What do you mean?"

"Think about it," Sabrina explained, her eyes sparkling with excitement. "A ghost dog who's been observing everything that happens in the diner? He's probably seen things we couldn't even imagine. And with his ability to sense distress and provide comfort, he could be an invaluable asset to our team."

Mort nodded, a grin spreading across his face. "A paranormal pup with a nose for trouble? I like the sound of that."

The ghost dog, as if understanding the weight of the moment, let out an excited bark, his ethereal tail wagging. Sabrina couldn't help but laugh, her heart swelling with affection for their newest ally.

"Well, little fella, it looks like you're officially part of the team now," she declared, giving the dog a gentle pat. "But you're going to need a name. How about... Boo?"

The dog's ears perked up at the sound of his new name, and he let out a joyful yip, prancing around the trio with a happy spring in his step. Sabrina, Mort, and Pepper exchanged glances, their faces a mix of amusement.

With Boo by their side, they knew they were one step closer to unraveling the mystery. And as the ghostly pup nuzzled against Sabrina's leg, she couldn't shake the feeling that this was just the beginning of a beautiful friendship – one that would change the course of their lives forever.

Sabrina clapped her hands together, a spark of excitement in her eyes. "Alright, team, let's get down to business. We've got a supernatural mystery to solve, and I have a feeling it's going to take all of our unique talents to crack this case wide open."

Spectres and Souffles

Mort leaned against the counter, his scythe glinting in the diner's fluorescent lights. "I've been around the block a few times when it comes to the afterlife, so I can definitely help navigate the spectral side of things. Plus, I've got a knack for getting information out of tight-lipped ghosts."

Pepper grinned, her fingers crackling with barely contained magical energy. "And I've got a few spells up my sleeve that might come in handy. They don't always go as planned, but when they do, they pack a serious punch!"

Boo let out a bark of agreement, his ghostly tail wagging with enthusiasm. Sabrina couldn't help but smile at the sight of her newly formed team, each member bringing something special to the table.

"I think we've got all the bases covered," she said. "Mort's expertise in the afterlife, Pepper's unpredictable magic, Boo's supernatural senses, and my own experience running this diner – we're like a paranormal dream team!"

But even as they reveled in their newfound unity, Sabrina knew that the real test was yet to come. With a celebrity chef cartel to investigate and a diner to protect, they would need all the help they could get.

She took a deep breath, her eyes scanning the faces of her teammates. "Pepper, Boo, I know we've only just met, but I can already tell that you're exactly what we need. I'd be honored if you'd join our team officially – not just for this case, but for whatever the future may bring."

Pepper's eyes widened, a mix of surprise and gratitude flickering across her face. "You really mean it, Sabrina? You want us to be a part of this, even with my unpredictable spells and Boo's, well, ghostliness?"

Sabrina reached out, placing a hand on Pepper's shoulder. "Absolutely. Your magic, no matter how chaotic, is a gift. And Boo's abilities are unlike anything I've ever seen. Together, we can achieve things that we never could alone."

As the reality of Sabrina's words sank in, Pepper and Boo exchanged a glance, a silent conversation passing between them. Then, with a shared nod and a grin, they turned back to Sabrina and Mort.

"We're in," Pepper declared, her voice ringing with conviction. "Let's show this cartel what happens when they mess with the Crossroads Diner!"

Boo let out a resounding bark of agreement, his ghostly form practically vibrating with excitement. And as the team stood together, united in their purpose, Sabrina couldn't help but feel a flicker of hope amidst the chaos.

They might be an unlikely bunch – a diner owner, a reaper on sabbatical, a witch with wayward spells, and a ghost dog – but together, they were unstoppable. And with the fate of the Crossroads Diner hanging in the balance, they knew that failure was not an option.

Sabrina leaned forward, her elbows resting on the diner's counter as she fixed her gaze on her newly formed team. "Alright, gang, it's time to get down to business. We need to figure out our next steps."

Mort nodded, his skeletal fingers tapping thoughtfully against his scythe. "Agreed. We can't just sit around waiting for the next supernatural attack. We need to be proactive."

"But where do we even start?" Pepper asked, her brows furrowed in concentration. "It's not like we have a lot to go on."

Sabrina pulled out a notepad and began jotting down ideas. "Well, we know that François's death is connected to this celebrity chef cartel somehow. I think our first step should be to gather more information about them – who they are, what they want, and how they operate."

Boo let out a soft whine, his ghostly tail wagging slowly. Sabrina smiled at him, understanding his unspoken concern. "Don't worry, Boo. We'll be careful. But we can't let fear hold us back from doing what's right."

Mort leaned forward, his eye sockets glowing. "I have some contacts in the afterlife who might be able to provide us with some intel. I'll reach out to them and see what I can find out."

Pepper's eyes sparkled with mischief. "And I can use my magic to do a little reconnaissance. A scrying spell here, a divination there – we'll have the dirt on these culinary creeps in no time!"

Sabrina looked around at her unlikely allies. "Thank you, all of you, for being here. I know we're up against some pretty powerful forces, but together, I believe we can overcome anything."

Spectres and Souffles

Mort grinned, his teeth gleaming in the diner's fluorescent lights. "Well, I don't know about you, but I'm ready to give these cartel clowns a taste of their own medicine. Let's show them."

With a resounding cheer, the team clinked their mugs together, sealing their pact. And as they sipped their coffee and plotted their next moves, the shadows outside the diner seemed to flicker and dance, as if the very fabric of the world was shifting in response.

Little did they know, their actions had not gone unnoticed. In a dark, smoky room on the other side of town, a figure sat hunched over a crystal ball, watching the scene unfold with narrowed eyes. "So," the figure murmured, their voice dripping with malice, "the Crossroads Diner has a new team of defenders. How... interesting."

The figure leaned back in their chair, a sinister smile playing at the corners of their mouth. "Let the games begin."

The morning sun peeked through the diner's windows, casting a warm glow on the bustling scene inside. Sabrina flitted about the kitchen, her dress swishing as she gathered an assortment of paranormal investigation tools: a spirit box, a set of divining rods, and a tattered grimoire filled with ancient spells.

"Pepper, have you seen my enchanted magnifying glass?" Sabrina called out, rummaging through a drawer.

Pepper looked up from her seat at the counter, where she was carefully inscribing runes onto a set of protection amulets. "I think I saw Mort using it to scratch his back earlier," she replied with a smirk.

Mort, who was lounging in a booth with his feet propped up on the table, let out an indignant snort. "I'll have you know, I was merely testing its magical properties. Can't have faulty equipment on our first mission, can we?"

Boo, the ghostly dog, phased through the wall and dropped the magnifying glass at Sabrina's feet, his spectral tail wagging with pride. Sabrina laughed and scratched behind his translucent ears. "Thanks, Boo. At least someone around here is helpful."

As the team gathered their supplies, an electric anticipation filled the air. Sabrina's heart raced with a mixture of excitement and nerves. This was it—their chance to prove themselves and protect the diner from the dark forces that threatened it.

Mort stood up and stretched, his bones creaking like old floorboards. "All right, team, let's get this show on the road. Those celebrity chef cartel goons won't know what hit 'em."

Pepper grinned. "I've got a few new spells up my sleeve that should give them a run for their money. They won't be able to resist my culinary enchantments!"

With their equipment packed and their spirits high, the team stepped out of the diner and into the unknown. The sun-dappled streets of the town stretched out before them, holding the promise of adventure and the threat of danger in equal measure.

As they walked, Sabrina couldn't shake the feeling that they were being watched. She glanced over her shoulder, but the street behind them was empty. Still, the hairs on the back of her neck stood on end, and a chill ran down her spine.

"Did you feel that?" she whispered to Mort, who was striding alongside her.

Mort nodded, his grim expression belying his usual sardonicism. "We're not alone," he murmured. "Someone, or something, is tracking our every move."

Pepper and Boo exchanged uneasy glances, their earlier bravado giving way to a growing sense of unease. The team pressed on, their footsteps echoing on the pavement as they ventured deeper into the heart of the town, unaware of the dark forces that lurked in the shadows, waiting to strike.

Little did they know, their every action was being monitored by a malevolent presence, one that sought to unravel the very fabric of the world they sought to protect. And as they rounded the corner, the figure in the smoky room leaned forward, their eyes glinting with malicious glee.

"Let the games begin, indeed," they whispered, their voice a sibilant hiss in the darkness. "Let's see how long these 'heroes' last before they crumble under the weight of their own hubris."

As the team delved deeper into the heart of the town, the once-familiar streets took on an eerie, otherworldly quality. The air grew thick with a palpable sense of unease, and the shadows seemed to dance with a life of their own. Sabrina's senses were on high alert, her every nerve ending tingling with the awareness of an unknown presence.

Spectres and Souffles

"We need to be careful," she murmured, her voice barely above a whisper. "I have a feeling we're walking into a trap."

Mort's eyes narrowed, his scythe at the ready. "Agreed. Keep your wits about you, and be prepared for anything."

Pepper's hands crackled with magical energy, her tattoos glowing with an otherworldly light. "I'm ready for whatever they throw at us," she declared.

Boo pressed close to Sabrina's side, his ghostly form shimmering in the moonlight. His nose twitched, and a low growl escaped his throat. "Something's coming," she warned. Boo's voice let out a throaty rumble.

Suddenly, the ground beneath their feet began to tremble, and a deafening roar filled the air. The team whirled around, their eyes widening in horror as a massive, twisted creature emerged from the shadows, its maw dripping with a viscous, black ichor.

"What in the name of all that's holy is that?" Pepper gasped, her voice trembling with fear.

Sabrina's heart raced, but she stood her ground. "I don't know, but we're not going to let it stop us," she declared, her voice ringing.

As the creature lumbered towards them, its eyes glowing with a malevolent red light, the team readied themselves for battle. Mort's scythe sliced through the air, Pepper's spells crackled with energy, and Boo's ghostly form shimmered with an otherworldly light.

But even as they fought, Sabrina couldn't shake the feeling this was more dangerous then she had thought. That the true mastermind behind the chaos was still out there, waiting in the shadows, ready to strike when they least expected it.

And as the creature fell to the ground, its body dissolving into a cloud of noxious smoke.

"We need to keep moving," she said.

The team nodded.

But little did they know, the figure in the smoky room was watching their every move, their lips curled in a twisted smile. "Impressive," they murmured, their voice filled with a dark amusement. "But let's see how long they last when the real games begin."

Chapter 7

The soft golden light of the setting sun streamed through the lace curtains of the Crossroads Diner's back room, casting a warm glow on the faces of the assembled team. Sabrina stood at the center of the room, her vintage dress swishing as she paced, her hazel eyes sparkling with determination.

"Alright team, we've got a mystery on our hands and a spirit to wrangle," she declared, her voice filled with a mix of excitement and urgency. "François is up to his old tricks again, and this time he's messing with the very heart of the Crossroads - the menu!"

Mort, the resident grim reaper, leaned against the wall, his bony fingers playing idly with the handle of his scythe. "So, what's the plan, boss? We gonna scare some sense into him?" His eye sockets glowed with mischief.

Sabrina shot him a playful glare. "Not quite, Mort. We're going to take a little field trip to the spirit realm and see if we can uncover any clues about François's motives."

Pepper, the resident witch with a penchant for miscast spells, bounced on her toes, her fiery red hair dancing around her face. "Ooh, an adventure! I'll pack some potions, just in case we run into any trouble." She grinned, her freckled nose crinkling with excitement.

Sabrina couldn't help but smile at Pepper's enthusiasm. The girl's optimism was infectious, even in the face of potential danger.

"Alright everyone, gather round," Sabrina instructed, extending her hands. "We're going to create a portal to the spirit realm. Focus your energy and hold on tight!"

Mort, Pepper, and Boo, Sabrina's faithful ghostly canine companion, formed a circle around her, their hands clasped together.

Spectres and Souffles

Sabrina closed her eyes, channeling her psychic energy as the room began to hum with an otherworldly resonance.

A shimmering, translucent portal materialized in the center of their circle, its edges pulsing with an ethereal light. The team exchanged glances, a mix of excitement and apprehension dancing in their eyes.

With a deep breath and a squeeze of their joined hands, Sabrina led her team through the portal, the diner fading away as they stepped into the swirling mists of the spirit realm.

As they stepped through the portal, the team was immediately enveloped in a shimmering mist, their surroundings transforming into a surreal landscape of swirling colors and floating orbs. The air felt thick with energy, tingling against their skin like a gentle electric current.

"Whoa," Pepper breathed. "This is incredible!"

Sabrina nodded, equally amazed by the ethereal beauty of the spirit realm. She had visited this plane before, but each time felt like a new adventure, full of surprises and mysteries waiting to be unraveled.

Mort, ever the skeptic, squinted at the floating orbs suspiciously. "Are we sure this is safe? I don't want to end up as some ghost's appetizer."

"Relax, Mort," Sabrina chuckled. "We'll be fine as long as we stick together and stay alert."

Boo yipped in agreement, his ghostly tail wagging excitedly as he bounded ahead, sniffing at the shimmering mist.

Suddenly, a mischievous voice cut through the ethereal silence. "Well, well, well, what do we have here? A group of adventurers, perhaps?"

The team whirled around to find a impish spirit floating before them, a playful grin stretching across his translucent face. His eyes sparkled with curiosity and a hint of mischief.

"Who are you?" Sabrina asked, her guard up but her tone friendly.

The spirit bowed with a flourish. "Jasper, at your service! And you must be the famous Sabrina Spellsworth, proprietor of the Crossroads Diner."

Sabrina raised an eyebrow, surprised by the spirit's knowledge of her identity. "How do you know who I am?"

Jasper winked. "Word travels fast in the spirit realm, my dear. Your culinary prowess is legendary, especially that apple pie of yours."

My apple pie? Sabrina thought, a smile tugging at her lips. *Well, well, it seems my reputation precedes me, even in the afterlife.*

"I'll tell you what," Jasper continued, floating closer to the group. "I'll guide you through the spirit realm and help you uncover the clues you seek. But in exchange, I want a taste of that famous apple pie. Deal?"

Sabrina glanced at her team, silently gauging their reactions. Mort shrugged, Pepper nodded enthusiastically, and Boo yipped in approval.

A spirit guide could be just what we need to navigate this strange world, Sabrina reasoned, her instincts telling her to trust Jasper.

"Deal," she agreed, extending her hand to the mischievous spirit. "But first, we have a mystery to solve."

Jasper grinned, his translucent hand passing through Sabrina's in a chilling handshake. "Then let's not waste any more time. Follow me, and I'll lead you deeper into the realm. But be warned, the spirit world is full of surprises!"

With that, Jasper darted ahead, his spectral form weaving through the floating orbs and shimmering mist. Sabrina and her team exchanged glances before setting off in pursuit, their hearts pounding with anticipation and their minds razor-sharp, ready to unravel the secrets of François's ghostly agenda.

As they followed Jasper deeper into the spirit realm, the swirling mist parted, revealing a sprawling spectral forest. Gnarled trees with translucent leaves loomed overhead, their branches reaching out like ghostly fingers. The air hummed with an otherworldly energy, and Sabrina felt a tingle run down her spine.

"Listen closely," Jasper whispered, his voice echoing through the eerie stillness. "The trees here hold secrets, whispers of the past and glimpses of the future."

Sabrina strained her ears, and to her amazement, she could hear faint murmurs emanating from the trees. Snippets of conversations, long-lost confessions, and cryptic prophecies drifted on the spectral breeze.

"Do you hear that?" Mort asked, his skeletal hand cupping his ear hole. "It's like a symphony of secrets!"

Pepper nodded, her ghostly eyes wide with wonder. "I never knew trees could talk. This is incredible!"

Spectres and Souffles

As they ventured further, Sabrina noticed something peculiar on the forest floor. Faint, shimmering footprints appeared and disappeared, hinting at the presence of unseen beings.

We're not alone here, Sabrina realized, a mixture of excitement and apprehension coursing through her. *There are other spirits roaming this forest, each with their own stories and secrets.*

Suddenly, the trees parted, and the group found themselves standing at the edge of a bustling spectral marketplace. Ghostly vendors hawked their wares from translucent stalls, offering everything from ethereal fruits that glowed like miniature moons to delicate pastries that seemed to dissolve into mist at the slightest touch.

"Welcome to the Spirit Bazaar!" Jasper announced with a flourish. "Here, you'll find all sorts of otherworldly delights and curious characters."

As Sabrina and her team marveled at the surreal sight, a friendly spirit with a warm smile approached them. "Hello there! I'm Amelia. I couldn't help but overhear your conversation earlier. Did you mention François?"

Sabrina's heart leaped. "Yes, we did! We're trying to uncover the mystery behind his ghostly antics at my diner. Do you know anything about him?"

Amelia's smile faded, replaced by a somber expression. "I do, indeed. Before his death, François was investigating a cartel of celebrity chefs. He believed they were up to something sinister, but he never got the chance to expose them."

Sabrina exchanged shocked glances with her team. *A celebrity chef cartel? That's definitely not what I was expecting!*

"Do you have any idea what they were up to?" Mort asked, his bony brow furrowed in concern.

Amelia shook her head. "I'm afraid not. But I do know that François was determined to uncover the truth. He said he had evidence hidden somewhere, but he never revealed its location."

Hidden evidence, Sabrina mused. *If we can find it, maybe we can finally understand François's motivations and put an end to his meddling.*

As the group pondered this new revelation, a sudden commotion erupted in the marketplace. Ghostly vendors began closing up their stalls in a hurry, and the air crackled with an ominous energy.

"Sabrina, look!" Pepper gasped, pointing to the far end of the bazaar.

There, emerging from the swirling mists, was a group of menacing spirits, their forms dark and twisted. They moved with purpose, their eyes fixated on Sabrina and her team.

"Oh no," Amelia whispered, fear etched on her face. "It's the cartel's enforcers. They must have sensed your presence here. You need to run, now!"

Sabrina's heart pounded as she grabbed Mort's hand, Pepper and Boo close behind. Jasper darted ahead, leading them away from the impending danger.

With the cartel's enforcers hot on their heels, Sabrina and her team raced deeper into the spectral unknown, their quest for answers taking a thrilling and perilous turn.

Jasper led the group through a series of narrow, winding alleys, the sounds of the pursuing enforcers echoing off the ethereal walls. Sabrina's mind raced as they navigated the labyrinthine paths, trying to make sense of the new information they had gleaned from Amelia.

"Mort, any ideas on how we can shake off these goons?" Sabrina panted, glancing over her shoulder at the approaching shadows.

The grim reaper chuckled darkly, his bony fingers tightening around his scythe. "Oh, I have a few tricks up my sleeve, my dear. But let's save those for a last resort, shall we?"

Pepper rolled her eyes, her ghostly form shimmering with exertion. "Less banter, more running, you two!"

Suddenly, Jasper veered sharply to the right, guiding them through a shimmering portal that seemed to appear out of nowhere. The group tumbled through, landing in a sprawling, otherworldly library. Towering shelves stretched as far as the eye could see, each one laden with countless glowing tomes and scrolls.

"Welcome to the Spirit Archive," Jasper announced, dusting off his spectral suit. "If there's any information on that celebrity chef cartel, it'll be here."

Sabrina's eyes widened in awe as she took in the vast repository of knowledge. She could feel the weight of countless secrets and mysteries thrumming in the air around them.

Spectres and Souffles

Mort stepped forward, his eye sockets glinting with an eerie light. "Well, then, let's get searching, shall we? These old bones are itching for a good mystery."

As the team split up to scour the shelves, Sabrina couldn't shake the feeling that they were on the precipice of something monumental. Each step deeper into the archive seemed to bring them closer to the truth, but also closer to an unknown danger that lurked just out of sight.

Little did she know, the secrets they were about to uncover would change everything they thought they knew about the spirit world—and themselves.

As the team delved deeper into the labyrinthine archive, their hopes began to dwindle. Each tome they pulled from the shelves yielded nothing more than ethereal recipes and ghostly anecdotes. Sabrina's brow furrowed as she replaced yet another useless volume, her frustration mounting.

"We've been at this for hours," Mort grumbled, his skeletal fingers drumming against a nearby shelf. "Maybe François was just being paranoid. Wouldn't be the first time."

Sabrina shook her head, unwilling to give up. "No, there has to be something here. François wouldn't have risked his afterlife for nothing."

Just then, a soft whine caught their attention. Boo stood at the end of a narrow aisle, his ghostly tail wagging excitedly. His nose twitched as he pawed at a small, hidden alcove, almost invisible among the towering shelves.

"What is it, boy?" Sabrina asked, hurrying over to the spectral dog. "Did you find something?"

As she knelt beside Boo, her eyes fell upon a dusty, leather-bound tome tucked away in the alcove. Its spine was emblazoned with the title "Culinary Conspiracies: Secrets of the Celebrity Chef Cartel" in shimmering, ethereal letters.

Sabrina's heart raced as she carefully extracted the book from its hiding place. "Guys, I think this is it," she breathed, her fingers trembling with anticipation.

The team gathered around as Sabrina gently opened the tome, its pages crackling with age and secrets. As she began to read, her eyes widened in disbelief.

"I can't believe this," she muttered, her voice tinged with anger. "The cartel has been using subpar ingredients, engaging in fraudulent practices, and charging exorbitant prices. They've been scamming people for years!"

Mort leaned in, his jaw clicking thoughtfully. "And François must have been on the verge of exposing them. No wonder they wanted him out of the picture."

Sabrina's mind raced as the pieces of the puzzle began to fall into place. The celebrity chef cartel had a lot to answer for, and she was determined to bring them to justice—both in the mortal world and the spirit realm.

"We need to get this information to the authorities," she declared.

They had uncovered a great evil. Sabrina closed the book with a soft thud, her fingers lingering on its weathered cover. "Hang on tight, everyone," she warned, a mischievous glint in her eye. "Things are about to get even more interesting."

A spectral figure materialized before them, its translucent form shimmering in the ethereal light of the Spirit Archive. The librarian's glare swept over the group, and Sabrina felt a chill run down her spine.

"You must leave at once," the librarian intoned, his voice echoing through the labyrinthine maze of bookshelves. "Your presence has attracted the attention of malevolent spirits, and they are coming for you."

Pepper's eyes widened, her tattoos glowing with an intense urgency. "We can't just abandon our mission," she protested, her hair whipping around her face as she shook her head.

Sabrina placed a comforting hand on Pepper's shoulder, with understanding. "We have what we need for now," she reassured her friend. "We'll come back when it's safer, but right now, we need to get out of here."

Boo let out a low whine, his ghostly tail tucked between his legs as he sensed the approaching danger. Mort nodded solemnly, his skeletal fingers tightening around his scythe. "Sabrina's right," he said, his voice tinged with a rare seriousness. "We're no good to anyone if we get trapped here."

The team hastily closed the book, taking mental notes of its location for future reference. The spectral librarian beckoned them to follow, leading them through a series of winding passages and hidden doorways.

As they raced through the Spirit Archive, Sabrina could feel the malevolent presence drawing closer, its icy tendrils reaching out to ensnare them. She focused on the exit portal, visualizing their escape back to the safety of the mortal world.

Just as the malevolent spirits were about to overtake them, the team burst through the exit portal, tumbling back into the physical realm. They landed in a heap on the floor of the Crossroads Diner's back room, their bodies tingling with residual energy from the spirit realm.

Sabrina gasped for air, her heart pounding in her chest as she struggled to regain her composure. She glanced around at her friends, relief washing over her as she realized they had all made it back safely.

"That was too close for comfort," Mort quipped, brushing imaginary dust off his robes. "I prefer my adventures without the risk of eternal imprisonment, thank you very much."

Pepper let out a breathless laugh, her adrenaline still pumping. "At least we got what we needed," she said, her eyes sparkling with excitement. "Now we can start putting the pieces together and take down that celebrity chef cartel."

Sabrina nodded. They had faced down the dangers of the spirit realm and emerged victorious.

As the team caught their breath, the diner's walls seemed to hum with anticipation, as if the very building itself knew that great things were on the horizon. Sabrina smiled, her heart swelling with pride.

Sabrina turned to Jasper, who hovered nearby with a mischievous grin on his face. "Jasper, I can't thank you enough for your help," she said, her voice filled with sincere gratitude. "Without you, we might never have found the information we needed."

Jasper's eyes twinkled with delight. "Ah, think nothing of it, my dear," he replied, waving a translucent hand. "But I do believe you promised me a slice of that famous apple pie of yours."

Sabrina laughed, her heart warming at the spirit's playful demeanor. "Of course, Jasper. I always keep my promises. The next time you visit the diner, I'll have a slice waiting just for you."

With a final wink and a flourish, Jasper vanished, leaving behind a faint scent of cinnamon and mischief. Sabrina turned to her team, "Alright, gang, let's get back to the diner. We've got a lot of work ahead of us."

As they stepped through the portal, the familiar sights and sounds of the Crossroads Diner welcomed them home. The jukebox crooned a lively tune, and the aroma of freshly brewed coffee mingled with the tantalizing scent of sizzling bacon. Sabrina inhaled deeply, the comforting smells grounding her in the present moment.

But there was no time to waste. With the knowledge they had gained from the Spirit Archive, Sabrina knew they had to act fast. She gathered her team around a corner booth, their heads huddled together as they pored over the notes they had taken.

"François may have been onto something big," Sabrina mused, her brow furrowed in concentration. "If we can expose the celebrity chef cartel's fraudulent practices, we might be able to put an end to their influence once and for all."

Mort nodded, "And maybe give François the peace he deserves," he added, his voice tinged with empathy.

Sabrina felt a surge of affection for her otherworldly friends. She glanced around the diner, taking in the eclectic mix of patrons, both living and dead, and felt a sense of purpose fill her heart.

As the sun began to set outside the diner's windows, casting a warm, golden glow across the checkered floor, Sabrina smiled. It was time to get to work, and she couldn't wait to see where this new adventure would take them.

Suddenly, the diner's door burst open, and a disheveled figure stumbled inside, gasping for breath. Sabrina's eyes widened as she recognized the ghost of a once-famous chef, his appearance a far cry from the polished persona he had once portrayed on television.

"Please," he rasped, his spectral form flickering in distress. "You have to help me. They're coming for me, and if they find out what I know..."

Spectres and Souffles

Before he could finish his sentence, a gust of icy wind tore through the diner, and the ghost vanished, leaving behind a chilling silence in his wake.

Sabrina exchanged a troubled glance with her team, her heart racing as she realized that their investigation had just taken a dangerous turn. The stakes had never been higher, and time was running out. They had to act fast, or risk losing everything they had worked so hard to uncover.

Mort's bony fingers tightened around the handle of his scythe as he spoke, his voice low and urgent. "We need to find out what that ghost knows, and fast. If the cartel is after him, they won't stop until they've silenced him for good."

Pepper nodded, body crackling with magical energy. "I can try to track his spectral signature, but we'll need to act quickly. The longer we wait, the colder the trail will get."

"Alright, team," Sabrina said, her voice steady and clear. "Let's gear up and head out. We've got a ghost to find and a cartel to take down."

As they gathered their supplies and prepared to leave, Boo let out a soft whine, his ghostly tail wagging nervously. Sabrina knelt down beside him, running her fingers through his translucent fur.

"Don't worry, Boo," she murmured, her voice soothing. "We'll keep each other safe, no matter what happens."

With a final glance around the diner, Sabrina led her team out into the gathering darkness, the cool night air.

The streets of the city were eerily quiet as they walked, the only sound the echoing tap of their footsteps against the pavement. Sabrina's senses were on high alert, her eyes scanning the shadows for any sign of danger.

Suddenly, Pepper stopped, her tattoos glowing a brilliant blue. "I've got something," she whispered, her voice tight with excitement. "The ghost's signature is coming from that abandoned warehouse up ahead."

Sabrina's heart raced as they approached the looming structure, its windows dark and its walls covered in peeling paint. She could feel the weight of the spirit realm pressing in around them, the boundaries between the living and the dead growing thinner with each passing moment.

As they stepped inside, the musty scent of forgotten things filled their nostrils, and the darkness seemed to close in around them. Sabrina reached out with her psychic senses, searching for any sign of the ghost they sought.

And then, she felt it - a faint flicker of spectral energy, coming from somewhere deep within the warehouse. She motioned for her team to follow, her footsteps muffled by the thick layer of dust that coated the floor.

But as they turned a corner, they found themselves face to face with a group of ghostly figures, their eyes glowing with malevolent intent. Sabrina's breath caught in her throat as she realized that they had walked straight into a trap, and the cartel had been waiting for them all along.

The ghostly figures advanced, their spectral forms shimmering with dark energy, and Sabrina knew that they were in for the fight of their lives.

As the first ghost lunged forward, Sabrina raised her hands.

Chapter 8

The warm aroma of freshly brewed coffee and sizzling bacon enveloped Sabrina and Ambrose as they slid into the worn red vinyl booth. Sabrina's dress swished as she settled, a playful contrast to Ambrose's tailored suit.

"I have to say, their apple pie is simply divine," Sabrina confessed, her eyes sparkling. "The flaky crust, the tender apples, the hint of cinnamon - it's like a warm hug from grandma herself!"

Ambrose chuckled, his blue eyes crinkling at the corners. "While I do appreciate a classic slice, I must admit, the truffle pasta I had in Italy was an otherworldly experience. The earthy aroma, the silky texture - it was like dancing across my taste buds."

"You know, this pie reminds me of baking with my grandmother as a little girl," Sabrina shared, a wistful smile playing on her lips. "She'd let me roll out the dough, my tiny hands covered in flour. Those moments in her cozy kitchen, the scent of cinnamon and love in the air - they're some of my most treasured memories."

Ambrose nodded, a flicker of vulnerability in his eyes. "I can relate. I once tried to impress a date by making a chocolate soufflé from scratch. Let's just say, it was less of a romantic dessert and more of a deflated disaster!" He laughed, the sound warm and genuine.

Sabrina giggled, picturing the debonair Ambrose covered in cocoa powder, frantically trying to salvage a sunken soufflé. *It's refreshing to see him let his guard down*, she thought, feeling a growing connection.

Their shared laughter mingled with the clinking of coffee mugs and the chatter of nearby patrons. For a moment, the weight of the mystery surrounding them seemed to lift, replaced by the simple joy of two kindred spirits bonding over their love of food and the memories it evoked.

But as Sabrina's gaze drifted to the bustling street outside the diner's window, a figure lurking in the shadows caught her eye. The man's fedora was pulled low, obscuring his face, but there was something unsettlingly familiar about his stance. A chill ran down her spine, the cozy warmth of the diner suddenly feeling far away...

Sabrina leaned in, a playful glint in her eye. "So, Mr. Saffron, I hear you're a fan of sous vide cooking. Isn't that just fancy talk for boiling food in a bag?"

Ambrose clutched his heart in mock offense. "I'll have you know, sous vide is a precise and delicate art form. It allows for unparalleled control over temperature and texture."

"Oh, please!" Sabrina laughed. "Give me a trusty cast iron skillet and some butter, and I'll show you what real cooking is all about."

Ambrose raised an eyebrow, a smirk tugging at the corner of his mouth. "Ah, the classic 'butter makes everything better' argument. While I can't deny the allure of a perfectly seared steak, there's something to be said for the science behind sous vide."

She couldn't help but be drawn to Ambrose's quick wit and the way his eyes sparkled when he spoke about cooking.

As their laughter subsided, Sabrina felt a heaviness settle in her chest. She toyed with the napkin in her lap, her smile faltering. "Ambrose, I..." She paused, searching for the right words. "I can't help but worry about what we're getting ourselves into. With François's death and all the unanswered questions surrounding it, I fear that digging deeper might put us in danger."

Ambrose's expression grew serious, his blue eyes intense. He reached across the table, his hand hovering near hers, a silent offer of support. "Sabrina, I understand your concerns. But I believe that together, we can unravel this mystery and bring the truth to light. We'll watch out for each other, every step of the way."

Sabrina's heart raced at his words, a mixture of fear and exhilaration coursing through her veins. She knew that embarking on this journey with Ambrose would change everything, but deep down, she also knew it was a path she had to follow.

As if on cue, the bell above the diner's door jingled, and a figure stepped inside, a gust of wind swirling around them. Sabrina's eyes widened as she recognized the newcomer - it was none other than the town's eccentric librarian, known for her vast knowledge of local history and her uncanny ability to appear just when she was needed most...

Sabrina's heart skipped a beat as she recognized the eccentric librarian, Minerva Quillworth, her silver hair piled high in a bun and her piercing green eyes scanning the diner. Minerva's presence always signaled a turning point in any mystery.

Minerva approached their booth, her long, flowing skirt swishing with each step. "Sabrina, Ambrose," she greeted them with a knowing smile. "I had a feeling I'd find you two here, deep in discussion about the recent... events."

Ambrose raised an eyebrow, his curiosity piqued. "Minerva, what brings you here on this blustery evening? Do you have any insights to share?"

The librarian slid into the booth beside Sabrina, the scent of old books and lavender enveloping them. "I may have stumbled upon some information that could shed light on your investigation," she said, her voice low and conspiratorial. "But first, I must know if you're truly prepared for the journey ahead."

Sabrina exchanged a glance with Ambrose, a silent understanding passing between them. She turned to Minerva, "We're ready," she said firmly.

Minerva nodded, a flicker of approval in her eyes. She reached into her satchel and withdrew a weathered leather-bound journal, placing it on the table between them. "This," she said, tapping the cover with a slender finger, "holds the key to unlocking the secrets of the celebrity chef cartel. But be warned, the path ahead is fraught with danger and deception."

Sabrina's pulse quickened as she stared at the journal. She glanced at Ambrose, who leaned forward, his eyes fixed on the mysterious tome. "We'll handle whatever comes our way," he said, his voice steady and reassuring.

As Minerva began to reveal the contents of the journal, Sabrina felt a surge of energy coursing through her.

The sun had already begun its descent, casting a warm golden glow through the library's tall windows as Sabrina and Ambrose pored over the contents of the mysterious journal. The musty scent of aged paper and well-worn leather filled their nostrils, a testament to the secrets hidden within its pages.

"Look at this," Sabrina whispered, her finger tracing a line of elegant script. "It mentions a secret society of chefs, bound together by a code of silence and a shared passion for culinary excellence."

Ambrose leaned closer, his brow furrowed in concentration. "And here," he said, pointing to a series of names and dates, "it seems they've been active for decades, influencing the world of haute cuisine from the shadows."

As they delved deeper into the journal, a sense of unease began to settle over Sabrina. The chefs' methods were shrouded in secrecy, and the journal hinted at a darker purpose behind their exclusive gatherings. She couldn't shake the feeling that François's death was somehow connected to this clandestine group.

Ambrose must have sensed her discomfort, for he reached out and gave her hand a reassuring squeeze. "We'll get to the bottom of this, Sabrina. Together."

She met his gaze, finding solace in the determination that shone in his eyes. "I just hope we're not in over our heads," she murmured, her mind drifting to the potential dangers that lay ahead.

As they continued their research, Sabrina and Ambrose discovered a series of cryptic clues scattered throughout the journal's pages. It was as if the author had anticipated the need for secrecy, encoding vital information in riddles and enigmatic references.

"It's like a treasure hunt," Ambrose mused, a hint of excitement in his voice. "Each clue leads us one step closer to the truth."

Sabrina nodded, "And the prize at the end is justice for François and the chance to expose the cartel's misdeeds."

They threw themselves into deciphering the clues, their combined knowledge and intuition guiding them through the labyrinthine mystery. As the hours ticked by, the library's silence was broken only by the occasional rustle of turning pages and the soft murmur of their voices as they traded theories and insights.

Just as the last rays of sunlight began to fade, Sabrina's eyes widened in realization. "I think I've got it," she breathed, her heart pounding. "The final piece of the puzzle."

Spectres and Souffles

Ambrose leaned in, "What does it say?"

Sabrina's voice trembled slightly as she read aloud the cryptic message: "In the den of the lion, where flavors dance and tempers flare, the truth shall be unveiled, and the master's fate laid bare."

A heavy silence settled over them as the implications of the clue sank in. They exchanged a knowing look, the unspoken understanding passing between them like an electric current.

"The Lion's Den," Ambrose said, his voice barely above a whisper. "The most exclusive restaurant in the city, known for its fiery head chef and his temper tantrums in the kitchen."

Sabrina nodded, a sense of foreboding washing over her. "And it's where François worked before he died."

As they gathered their notes and prepared to leave the library, Sabrina couldn't shake the feeling that they were on the cusp of something momentous. The truth was within their grasp, but so too were the dangers that lurked in the shadows of the culinary world.

With a deep breath and a resolute nod, Sabrina and Ambrose stepped out into the gathering dusk and the unraveling of the celebrity chef cartel's dark secrets.

As the sun dipped below the horizon, painting the sky in hues of orange and pink, Sabrina and Ambrose made their way through the bustling streets of the city. The Lion's Den loomed ahead, its imposing façade a stark contrast to the warmth of the fading daylight.

Sabrina's heart raced as they approached the restaurant's entrance, the weight of their discovery pressing down on her like a physical force. She glanced at Ambrose, finding comfort in his steady presence beside her.

"Ready?" he asked, his hand resting on the polished brass handle of the door.

Sabrina nodded. "As ready as I'll ever be."

They stepped inside, the rich aroma of simmering sauces and sizzling meats enveloping them like a warm embrace. The maître d' greeted them with a practiced smile, his eyes flickering with recognition as they landed on Ambrose.

"Ah, Mr. Saffron," he said, his voice smooth as silk. "We've been expecting you."

Ambrose raised an eyebrow, his posture stiffening almost imperceptibly. "Have you now?"

The maître d' nodded, gesturing for them to follow him. "The chef has prepared a special menu for you tonight. He insists on personally overseeing your dining experience."

Sabrina and Ambrose exchanged a look, the unease palpable between them. They followed the maître d' through the dimly lit restaurant, the buzz of conversation and clinking of cutlery fading into the background as they were led deeper into the heart of the Lion's Den.

As they passed through the swinging doors that separated the dining room from the kitchen, Sabrina's senses were assaulted by a cacophony of sounds and smells. Chefs barked orders, pots and pans clanged, and the sizzle of food on the stove filled the air.

In the center of the chaos stood a man, his white chef's coat pristine amidst the frenzy of activity. He turned to face them, his eyes glinting with a mixture of amusement and malice.

"Welcome, Mr. Saffron," he said, his voice carrying over the din of the kitchen. "And you must be the lovely Sabrina Spellsworth. I've heard so much about you."

Sabrina's blood ran cold as she realized the trap they had walked into. The chef's smile widened, a predatory gleam in his eyes as he stepped forward, a gleaming knife held loosely in his hand.

"I believe it's time we had a little chat about your meddling in my business," he said, the threat in his words as sharp as the blade he wielded. "And I promise you, it's a conversation you won't soon forget."

Sabrina's heart raced as she faced the menacing chef, her mind frantically searching for a way out of this dangerous situation. Ambrose stepped forward, his body tense and ready for action.

"I think there's been a misunderstanding," he said, his voice calm and even. "We're just here to enjoy a meal, not cause any trouble."

The chef laughed, a harsh, grating sound that echoed off the metal surfaces of the kitchen. "Don't play coy with me, Mr. Saffron. I know exactly why you're here, and I won't let you interfere with my plans."

Sabrina's eyes darted around the kitchen, taking in the positions of the other chefs, the layout of the room, and the potential weapons at their disposal. She leaned closer to Ambrose, her voice low and urgent.

"We need to get out of here, now," she whispered, her breath hot against his ear. "I have an idea, but we'll have to work together."

Ambrose nodded almost imperceptibly, his trust in Sabrina unwavering. "Lead the way," he murmured, his hand brushing against hers in a gesture of support.

Sabrina took a deep breath, steeling herself for what was to come. She focused her energy, reaching out with her mind to the spirits that lingered in the kitchen, the ghosts of chefs past who had poured their hearts and souls into their culinary creations.

"Help us," she pleaded silently, her voice echoing through the ethereal realm.

The air around them shimmered, the temperature dropping as spectral forms began to take shape. The ghostly chefs surrounded Sabrina and Ambrose, their translucent bodies forming a protective barrier between them and their adversary.

The living chef's eyes widened in shock and fear as he witnessed the supernatural display, his knife clattering to the floor as he stumbled backward. Sabrina seized the opportunity, grabbing Ambrose's hand and pulling him towards the exit, the ghostly chefs parting like a curtain to let them pass.

They burst through the swinging doors, their hearts pounding in their chests as they raced through the restaurant, the startled patrons gawking at their frenzied escape. They emerged into the cool night air, gulping down deep breaths as they tried to regain their composure.

"That was too close," Ambrose panted, his hand still clasped tightly in Sabrina's. "We need to regroup and come up with a new plan. We can't keep stumbling into these dangerous situations unprepared."

Sabrina acknowledged. "You're right," she said,. "We need to be smart about this, gather more information.

They walked hand in hand into the night, the stars twinkling overhead as they plotted their next move.

Chapter 9

Sabrina's fingers trembled as she stared at the crumpled letter in her hands, the world around her fading into a distant blur. Hidden beneath a stack of culinary magazines in Ambrose's office, the inconspicuous envelope had caught her eye, and now its contents threatened to shatter everything she thought she knew about the enigmatic food critic.

"No, this can't be right," she muttered under her breath, her eyes scanning the page for the tenth time. The words "Celebrity Chef Cartel" and "confidential arrangement" seemed to mock her from the paper, each line a damning indictment of Ambrose's true nature.

Sabrina's mind raced as she tried to reconcile the charming, sophisticated man she'd grown so fond of with the shadowy figure implicated in the letter. The diner's cheerful buzz suddenly felt suffocating, the once-comforting aroma of freshly brewed coffee now tinged with an acrid aftertaste.

She took a deep, steadying breath, straightening her polka-dot dress as she steeled herself for the confrontation to come. With the letter clutched tightly in her hand, Sabrina marched out of the office, her heels clicking purposefully against the checkered floor.

Ambrose looked up from his plate of eggs Benedict as she approached, a warm smile playing at the corners of his lips. "Sabrina, my dear, I was just savoring the exquisite hollandaise sauce. You've truly outdone yourself this morning."

Sabrina slapped the letter down on the table, her hazel eyes flashing with a mixture of hurt and anger. "Cut the small talk, Ambrose. What is this?"

His smile faltered, a flicker of unease crossing his chiseled features. "I'm afraid I don't know what you're referring to..."

Spectres and Souffles

"Don't play dumb with me," Sabrina snapped, her voice rising above the diner's chatter. "This letter, hidden in your office. It links you to the Celebrity Chef Cartel. The same cartel that's been causing chaos in the culinary world. The same cartel that might be responsible for François's death!"

Ambrose's eyes widened, his normally composed demeanor cracking under the weight of her accusation. "Sabrina, please, let me explain—"

"Explain what? That you've been lying to me this whole time? That our entire... relationship has been based on deceit?" She choked on the word, her heart constricting painfully in her chest.

Was it all a lie? Sabrina wondered, searching Ambrose's face for any hint of the man she thought she knew. The shared laughs, the stolen glances, the undeniable connection... could it have been nothing more than a carefully crafted façade?

"It's not what you think," Ambrose insisted, his voice low and urgent. "There's more to this than meets the eye."

Sabrina shook her head, tears stinging the corners of her eyes. "I trusted you, Ambrose. I let you into my life, into my heart. And now I find out that you're involved with the very people who might have murdered one of my dearest friends?"

She turned away, unable to bear the sight of him any longer. *How could I have been so blind?* she berated herself. *So foolish to believe that someone like Ambrose could ever truly care for me.*

"Sabrina, wait!" Ambrose called after her, his chair scraping against the floor as he stood to follow.

But Sabrina was already gone, the letter crumpled in her fist as she fled the diner, her heart shattered and her world turned upside down. The truth, it seemed, was far more bitter than she could have ever imagined.

Sabrina burst into the kitchen, startling Pepper and Boo, who were engrossed in a heated debate about the proper way to fold napkins. Mort, ever-present and all-knowing, hovered nearby, his skeletal face somehow conveying a mixture of concern and amusement.

"Sabrina, darling, what's wrong?" Pepper asked, her usually cheerful demeanor replaced by a frown. "You look like you've seen a ghost... and not one of the friendly ones."

Boo yipped in agreement.

"Did something happen with Ambrose?"

Sabrina slumped against the counter, the letter still clutched in her hand. "I found this," she said, her voice barely above a whisper. "It's a letter connecting Ambrose to the celebrity chef cartel."

Mort drifted closer, his dark robes billowing around him. "Well, well, well," he drawled, his eye sockets glowing with intrigue. "It seems our dear Ambrose has been keeping secrets."

"I confronted him about it," Sabrina continued, her eyes distant and pained. "He denied everything, claimed it was all a misunderstanding. But I don't know what to believe anymore."

Pepper wrapped a comforting arm around Sabrina's shoulders. "Oh, honey, I'm so sorry. But you know what they say: the truth will set you free... even if it hurts like hell."

Sabrina managed a weak smile, grateful for the support of her otherworldly friends. "Thanks, guys. I just... I need to know the truth. I need to find out if Ambrose is really who I thought he was."

Mort rubbed his bony hands together, a wicked grin spreading across his skeletal features. "And that, my dear, is where we come in. We'll dig up every dirty little secret Ambrose has buried, and we'll make sure justice is served... one way or another."

Sabrina took a deep breath, steeling herself for the task at hand. "Okay, team. Let's start with Ambrose's former colleagues. Mort, can you and Pepper dig up any dirt on his past jobs, see if there were any red flags or suspicious behavior?"

Mort grinned, his skeletal fingers tapping together eagerly. "Consider it done, boss. We'll rattle a few chains and see what skeletons come tumbling out of Ambrose's closet."

Pepper nodded, her ghostly form shimmering with determination. "I'll float around, eavesdrop on some conversations. You'd be surprised how much people let slip when they think no one's listening."

Sabrina turned to Mort, her eyebrows raised in question. "Mort, do you think you could use your connections to look into Ambrose's financials? See if there's anything that doesn't add up?"

Mort puffed out his chest, his translucent form swelling with pride. "Leave it to me, Sabrina. I'll haunt every bank and accounting firm in town until I find something. If Ambrose has been cooking the books, I'll sniff it out like a bloodhound on a scent trail."

Spectres and Souffles

As her friends set off on their respective missions, Sabrina retreated to her office, her mind racing with possibilities. She pulled out the letter that had started it all, studying the cryptic messages exchanged between Ambrose and the cartel members.

Hours turned into days as Sabrina and her team worked tirelessly to uncover the truth. Pepper returned with tales of Ambrose's past indiscretions, of shady dealings and questionable associations. Mort materialized in Sabrina's office, his face grim as he presented her with a stack of financial records that painted a picture of corruption and deceit.

Sabrina's heart sank with each new revelation, the weight of Ambrose's betrayal crushing her spirit. She pored over the evidence, connecting the dots between Ambrose and the cartel, her doubts solidifying into a cold, hard certainty.

He lied to me, she realized, tears stinging her eyes. *He looked me in the face and lied, even as the proof of his guilt was staring me right in the eye.*

But even as her heart broke, Sabrina knew she couldn't let her feelings cloud her judgment. She had a duty to the truth, to the memory of François, and to the countless others who had fallen victim to the cartel's machinations.

With a heavy sigh, Sabrina gathered the damning evidence, her resolve hardening with each passing moment. She would confront Ambrose, demand answers, and see that justice was served on a silver platter...

Sabrina stormed into Ambrose's office, the incriminating evidence clutched tightly in her trembling hands. Ambrose looked up from his desk, his eyes widening as he took in her fierce expression and the damning papers she held.

"Sabrina, my dear, what brings you here at this late hour?" Ambrose asked, his tone a mix of surprise and trepidation.

"Don't you 'my dear' me, Ambrose," Sabrina snapped, slamming the evidence down on his desk. "I know everything. The financial records, the cryptic messages, your involvement with the cartel. It's all here, in black and white."

Ambrose's face paled, his usually composed demeanor crumbling under the weight of Sabrina's accusations. He rose from his chair, hands held out in a placating gesture. "Sabrina, please, let me explain. It's not what it looks like."

"Really?" Sabrina scoffed, her voice dripping with sarcasm. "Because it looks like you've been lying to me, to everyone, about your true nature. How could you, Ambrose? How could you betray my trust, betray everything we've built together?"

Ambrose's shoulders slumped, his eyes filled with a mixture of guilt and desperation. "I never meant to hurt you, Sabrina. You have to believe me. I was caught in a web of my own making, trapped by the cartel's threats and demands."

Sabrina's heart clenched, her anger momentarily tempered by a flicker of empathy. *Could this be true?* she wondered, searching Ambrose's face for any sign of deception. *Could he have been coerced, forced to act against his will?*

But the evidence was damning, and Sabrina knew she couldn't let her feelings cloud her judgment. "I want the truth, Ambrose," she demanded, her voice firm despite the tears that threatened to fall. "No more lies, no more secrets. Tell me everything, or I walk away and never look back."

Ambrose closed his eyes, his face etched with pain and regret. When he spoke, his voice was barely above a whisper. "You're right, Sabrina. I've been living a lie, caught in a web of my own making. The cartel... they approached me years ago, when I was just starting out as a critic. They offered me money, influence, everything I thought I wanted. But the price... the price was too high."

Sabrina listened, her heart breaking with each revelation. She could see the anguish in Ambrose's eyes, the weight of his guilt bearing down on him like a physical burden.

"I tried to break free," Ambrose continued, his voice raw with emotion. "But they threatened me, threatened to ruin my reputation, to hurt the people I cared about. I was a coward, Sabrina. I chose my own safety over what was right, and I've regretted it every day since."

Sabrina's mind reeled, torn between her feelings for Ambrose and the bitter sting of his betrayal. She knew she had a choice to make, a decision that would shape the course of her life and the lives of those she held dear.

Spectres and Souffles

Do I turn him in? she wondered, her heart heavy with the weight of her responsibility. *Or do I help him find redemption, to make amends for his past mistakes?*

As she looked into Ambrose's eyes, seeing the genuine remorse and the flicker of hope that still burned within, Sabrina knew that the path forward would be far from easy. But she also knew that she couldn't turn her back on him, not when there was still a chance for him to make things right.

"We have a lot to talk about," she said softly, reaching out to take Ambrose's hand in her own. "But first, we need to figure out how to bring down the cartel, once and for all."

Sabrina turned to her loyal friends, her eyes searching their faces for guidance and support. Mort, his skeletal features softened by the gentle glow of the candlelight, stepped forward, his voice a reassuring whisper in the stillness of the room.

"Sabrina, my dear," he said, his words tinged with the wisdom of the ages, "the path to redemption is never an easy one, but it is a path worth taking. Ambrose may have stumbled, but he is not beyond hope."

Pepper, nodded in agreement. "Sabrina, you have the strength within you to face this challenge," she said, her words infused with the magic of her unwavering belief. "You've never been one to back down from a fight, especially when it comes to protecting those you love."

Boo, silent but steadfast, placed a comforting hand on Sabrina's shoulder, his touch a reminder of the unbreakable bonds of friendship that had seen them through countless trials and tribulations.

She turned to Ambrose, her voice steady and clear. "We'll face this together," she said, her words a promise and a vow. "But first, we need a plan. The cartel won't go down without a fight, and we'll need all the help we can get."

Ambrose nodded. "I'll do whatever it takes," he said, his voice a solemn oath. "I won't let you down again, Sabrina. I swear it."

Sabrina found herself in a dimly lit alleyway, the cold night air nipping at her skin as she waited for her contact from the cartel. She fidgeted with the hem of her vintage dress, wondering if her usual charming attire might be a bit too conspicuous for this clandestine meeting. *Well, it's too late to change now,* she thought wryly, *unless I want to risk being fashionably late to my own sting operation.*

She closed her eyes for a moment, reaching out with her mind to the spirits that always seemed to linger nearby. *If you're out there*, she called silently, *I could really use your help tonight. Any intel on the cartel would be much appreciated.*

As if in response, a sudden gust of wind whipped through the alley, carrying with it a series of whispers and murmurs that only Sabrina could hear. She strained to make out the words, her brow furrowed in concentration.

The warehouse on the pier... a shipment coming in tonight... the boss will be there...

Sabrina's eyes snapped open, a triumphant grin spreading across her face. *Bingo,* she thought, *that's exactly the kind of information I needed.*

Just then, a figure emerged from the shadows, his face obscured by a wide-brimmed hat and a high-collared coat. Sabrina straightened her shoulders and stepped forward, her voice calm and confident as she spoke.

"I hear you're the one to talk to about joining the cartel," she said, her tone casual and just a bit conspiratorial. "I've got some skills that I think your boss might find useful."

The figure looked her up and down, his eyes narrowing suspiciously. "And what skills might those be, Miss...?"

"Spellsworth," Sabrina replied smoothly, extending her hand in greeting. "Sabrina Spellsworth. And let's just say I have a way of getting information that others can't. A sixth sense, you might call it."

The man hesitated for a moment before shaking her hand, his grip firm and unyielding. "We'll see about that," he said gruffly. "The boss doesn't take kindly to outsiders, especially ones who claim to have special abilities."

You have no idea, Sabrina thought, suppressing a smirk. Out loud, she simply nodded and said, "I understand. But I assure you, my abilities are quite real. And I'm willing to prove it, if given the chance."

The man studied her for a long moment, his expression unreadable. Finally, he nodded curtly and gestured for her to follow him. "Come with me," he said, his voice low and ominous. "But be warned,

Miss Spellsworth. If you're playing games, you won't like the consequences."

Sabrina took a deep breath and fell into step beside him. She was walking a dangerous line, and one misstep could spell disaster for her and everyone she cared about. But she knew that she had no choice. The cartel had to be stopped, and she was the only one who could do it.

Sabrina found herself in a dimly lit room, the air heavy with the scent of cigar smoke and expensive cologne. The man who had led her there, a hulking figure with a scar across his cheek, lounged in a leather armchair, his eyes fixed on her with a predatory intensity.

"So," he drawled, "you claim to have information about our little operation. Information that could be very valuable to us."

Sabrina nodded, forcing a confident smile. "That's right. I've been doing some digging, and let's just say I've uncovered some things that could make life very difficult for you and your associates."

The man leaned forward, his eyes narrowing. "And what, exactly, do you want in return for this supposed information?"

Play it cool, Sabrina, she told herself, *don't let him see you sweat.* "I want in," she said, her voice steady. "I want a piece of the action. And I want protection. You take care of me, and I'll make sure your secrets stay buried."

The man studied her for a long moment, his expression unreadable. Then, without warning, he burst into laughter, the sound harsh and mocking. "You've got guts, kid, I'll give you that. But do you really think we're going to let some two-bit psychic into our inner circle just because she claims to have dirt on us?"

Sabrina's heart sank, but she refused to let it show. "I'm not just any psychic," she said, her voice low and intense. "I have abilities that you can't even begin to understand. And trust me, the information I have is the real deal."

The man's laughter died away, replaced by a cold, calculating look. "Is that so?" he said, his voice dangerously soft. "Well then, perhaps you'd like to give us a little demonstration of these abilities of yours."

Oh, crap, Sabrina thought, her mind racing. *I didn't plan for this.* But she knew she couldn't back down now.

She closed her eyes, reaching out with her mind to the spirits that always seemed to linger just beyond the veil. *Please,* she thought desperately, *if any of you are listening, I could really use some help right now.*

For a moment, there was nothing. Then, suddenly, she felt a presence beside her, a ghostly figure that only she could see. It was a man, tall and gaunt, with a face that seemed to be nothing but shadows.

"Tell him," the spirit whispered, its voice like the rustle of dry leaves, "that his partner is plotting to betray him. That he has been skimming money from the operation and plans to disappear with it all."

Sabrina's eyes snapped open, and she fixed the scarred man with a triumphant stare. "Your partner," she said, her voice ringing with conviction, "the one with the tattoo of a snake on his arm. He's been stealing from you. And he's planning to run off with everything, leaving you to take the fall."

The man's face went pale, his eyes widening in shock. "How...how could you possibly know that?" he stammered, his composure cracking.

Sabrina shrugged, feeling a rush of exhilaration. "I told you," she said coolly, "I have my ways. Now, do we have a deal, or not?"

The man stared at her for a long moment, his jaw clenched tight. Then, slowly, he nodded. "Alright," he said, his voice grudging. "You're in. For now. But you'd better pray that your information is as good as you claim. Because if it's not...well, let's just say that you'll be joining your ghostly friends a lot sooner than you'd like."

Sabrina's smile never wavered, but inside, she felt a chill run down her spine.

Sabrina burst into the diner, her heart still racing from her close call with the cartel. Mort, Pepper, and Boo looked up in surprise, their faces etched with worry.

"Sabrina!" Mort exclaimed, rushing over to her. "Are you alright? What happened?"

Spectres and Souffles

Sabrina took a deep breath, trying to steady herself. "I'm fine," she said, her voice shaking slightly. "But we have a problem. A big problem."

She quickly filled them in on what had transpired at the meeting, the words tumbling out of her in a rush. When she was finished, the others stared at her in stunned silence.

"I can't believe it," Pepper said at last, her voice hushed. "You actually infiltrated the cartel. And they bought your story about being a psychic."

Sabrina nodded, a wry smile tugging at her lips. "Apparently, I'm more convincing than I thought. But now comes the hard part. We have to find a way to expose them, and fast. Before they realize that I'm not really on their side."

Boo frowned, his ghostly brow furrowed in thought. "But how?" he asked, his voice echoing strangely in the empty diner. "They're not just going to let you waltz in and start snooping around."

Sabrina's smile turned grim. "No, they're not. Which is why we're going to have to get creative. And why we're going to need Ambrose's help, whether he likes it or not."

Poor Ambrose, she thought, her heart clenching at the thought of him. *He's in deeper than he ever could have imagined.*

She turned to the others. "Alright, team," she said, her voice ringing with conviction. "We've got a critic to save. And we're not going to stop until we've done both."

Mort and Pepper nodded, their own expressions mirroring her resolve. They knew the odds were stacked against them, but they also knew that they had no choice.

And with a little luck and a lot of guts, Sabrina thought, *maybe, just maybe, we'll come out of this in one piece.*

And with Ambrose by my side, where he belongs.

As the team huddled around the diner's counter, Sabrina pulled out a crumpled piece of paper from her apron pocket. "Okay, here's what we know," she said, smoothing out the paper. "The cartel's got their fingers in every high-end restaurant in the city, and they're not going to let anyone get in their way."

Mort leaned in, his ghostly form flickering in the diner's neon lights. "So, what's the plan, boss? We can't exactly go in guns blazing."

Sabrina chuckled, despite the gravity of the situation. "No, we can't. But we can go in with something better: information."

She tapped the paper, revealing a list of names and addresses. "These are all the restaurants we know are connected to the cartel. If we can get inside and find some hard evidence, we can take them down from the inside."

Pepper, ever the skeptic, raised an eyebrow. "And how exactly are we supposed to do that? It's not like we can just walk in and start snooping around."

Sabrina's eyes sparkled with mischief. "No, but we can send in someone they'll never suspect. Someone they trust."

She turned to Boo, the resident ghost dog, who was happily chewing on a spectral bone. "Boo, my furry friend, how do you feel about going undercover?"

Boo looked up, his tail wagging excitedly. "Ruff!" he barked, which Sabrina took as a resounding yes.

This is either going to be the most brilliant plan I've ever had, she thought, *or the most disastrous. But either way, it's the only chance we've got.*

She took a deep breath, steeling herself for what was to come. "Alright, gang," she said, her voice filled with a mixture of nerves and excitement. "Let's get this show on the road. We've got a critic to save and a cartel to take down, and we're not going to let anything stop us."

Chapter 10

The tantalizing aroma of freshly brewed coffee mingled with the lingering scent of Sabrina's famous cherry pie as the team huddled around the worn oak table in the back room of the Diner. Sunlight streamed through the lace-curtained window, casting a warm glow on their determined faces.

Sabrina leaned forward, her vintage dress crinkling with the movement. "We're running out of time. The culinary cartel is tightening its grip on the town, and if we don't expose them soon, the Crossroads Diner might become a ghost town itself."

Mort, his skeletal fingers wrapped around a chipped mug, chuckled darkly. "Well, that would certainly make my job easier. More souls to reap and all that."

Sabrina shot him a withering look. "This is serious, Mort. We need a plan."

Pepper, her fiery hair tied back in a messy bun, tapped her fingers on the table, sending tiny sparks dancing across the surface. "I say we use my magic to uncover their secrets. A little truth serum in their morning coffee should do the trick."

Boo, curled up under the table, let out a bark of agreement, his ghostly tail wagging enthusiastically.

Sabrina smiled at her loyal companions, feeling a swell of affection. They were an odd bunch, but she couldn't imagine facing this challenge without them. "I appreciate the enthusiasm, Pepper, but we need to be subtle. I think our best bet is to reach out to our ghostly patrons. They've been around long enough to know where the bodies are buried, metaphorically speaking."

Mort leaned back in his chair, the wood creaking under his ethereal weight. "I could also use my connections in the afterlife. You'd be surprised how chatty some of the recently deceased can be, especially when they've got a bone to pick with the living."

Sabrina knew they were up against a formidable foe, but with her team's unique abilities, they just might have a chance.

Suddenly, the back door burst open, and a gust of chilling wind swept through the room, rattling the cups and saucers on the table. In the doorway stood a ghostly figure, his translucent form flickering in the sunlight. Sabrina recognized him as one of her regular patrons, a former chef who had met an untimely end.

"Sabrina," he rasped, his voice echoing with an otherworldly timbre. "You must hurry. The cartel is planning something big, and if you don't stop them, the Crossroads Diner will be nothing more than a distant memory."

With those ominous words, the specter vanished, leaving the team stunned and more determined than ever to unravel the culinary cartel's sinister plot.

The musty scent of aged paper and well-worn leather enveloped Sabrina and her team as they stepped into the town's library. Towering shelves, laden with countless tomes, stretched towards the ceiling, casting long shadows across the hardwood floor. Sabrina inhaled deeply, finding comfort in the familiar aroma that transported her back to countless hours spent researching the paranormal.

"Well, if it isn't Sabrina Spellsworth and her merry band of misfits," a sharp voice cut through the tranquil atmosphere. Mrs. Jenkins, the librarian, peered at them over her wire-rimmed glasses, her steely gaze sizing up each member of the group.

Sabrina flashed her most disarming smile. "Mrs. Jenkins, you're looking as radiant as ever. We were hoping you could help us with a little research project."

The librarian's eyebrow arched skeptically. "Research? On what, pray tell? How to properly season a ghost pepper?"

Pepper, unable to resist a witty retort, chimed in, "Actually, I've got that covered. We're more interested in the culinary cartel that's been causing trouble around town."

Mrs. Jenkins' expression shifted, a flicker of unease passing over her features. "I'm not sure what you're talking about, dear. Perhaps you should stick to the cookbooks and leave the detective work to the professionals."

Undeterred, Sabrina pressed on. "We have reason to believe that the cartel is connected to some pretty high-profile chefs. Any information you could provide would be invaluable."

The librarian's gaze darted around the room, as if checking for eavesdroppers. "Fine," she relented, her voice dropping to a conspiratorial whisper. "But you didn't hear it from me. Try looking in the culinary history section, behind the row of cookbooks. You might find something... enlightening."

With a curt nod, Mrs. Jenkins turned on her heel and disappeared into the labyrinth of shelves. Sabrina exchanged a triumphant grin with her team, their excitement palpable.

"Alright, gang, let's split up and search. Pepper, you and Boo take the left side. Mort and I will tackle the right. If you find anything, give a shout."

As they dispersed, Sabrina couldn't shake the feeling that they were on the precipice of a major breakthrough. Her fingers trailed along the spines of countless books, their weathered covers whispering secrets of the past.

Suddenly, Mort's voice cut through the quiet. "Sabrina, over here! I think I found something."

She hurried to his side, her heart pounding with anticipation. Mort held a dusty tome, its cover emblazoned with the title "Secrets of the Culinary Underworld." With trembling hands, Sabrina flipped through the pages scanning the contents.

"This is it," she breathed. "It's all here—the cartel's operations, the chefs involved, everything."

Pepper joined them, peering over Sabrina's shoulder at the damning evidence. "We've got them now," Pepper declared, her tattoos glowing with renewed vigor.

But even as they reveled in their discovery, a nagging doubt tugged at the back of Sabrina's mind. Something about this felt too easy, too convenient. She couldn't shake the feeling that they were being watched, that the culinary cartel was always one step ahead.

As if on cue, a shadow detached itself from the shelves, a figure cloaked in darkness. Sabrina's breath caught in her throat, her ghostly senses screaming a warning. The figure moved towards them, a menacing aura emanating from its very being.

"Well, well, well," a sinister voice drawled. "What do we have here? A group of meddling do-gooders, sticking their noses where they don't belong."

Sabrina and her team found themselves face to face with a nightmare, a dark specter that threatened to unravel everything they had worked so hard to achieve. With a chill running down her spine, Sabrina realized that their battle against the culinary cartel had only just begun.

Sabrina's heart raced as she locked eyes with the shadowy figure, a librarian assistant whose very presence exuded an aura of malevolence. The spirit world whispered warnings in her ear, confirming her suspicions—this was no ordinary librarian.

"I suggest you put that book back where you found it," the cartel member hissed, his voice dripping with venom. "Unless you want to find out what happens to those who stick their noses where they don't belong."

Mort subtly positioned himself between the threat and his friends, his scythe glinting in the dim library light. "I think we'll hold onto it, thanks," he quipped, his skeletal grin unwavering.

Pepper's fingers twitched, ready to unleash a spell at a moment's notice. Boo's hackles rose, a low growl rumbling in his ghostly throat.

The cartel member's eyes narrowed, his hand slipping beneath his librarian's desk. Sabrina's breath hitched, fearing the worst. But before the situation could escalate, Pepper's mischievous grin widened.

"I think it's time for a little distraction," she whispered, her tattoos glowing with arcane power. With a flick of her wrist, a cascade of books flew from the shelves, swirling around the cartel member in a dizzying vortex of pages and dust.

"Now!" Sabrina yelled, clutching the incriminating tome to her chest as they made a break for the exit.

They burst out of the library, the cool evening air a welcome relief from the suffocating tension inside. Sabrina's heart pounded in her ears as they raced down the steps, putting as much distance between themselves and the cartel member as possible.

Spectres and Souffles

Finally, when they were sure they weren't being followed, they came to a stop, gulping in lungfuls of air. Sabrina leaned against a lamppost, the book still clutched tightly in her hands.

"That was too close," she panted, the adrenaline slowly subsiding. "We need more than just this book if we're going to take down the cartel."

Mort nodded, his bony fingers stroking his chin thoughtfully. "I might know a few spirits in the afterlife who could help us out. They've got dirt on everyone, even the culinary underworld."

Pepper's heart raced. "And I've got a few magical tricks up my sleeve that could come in handy. We'll need all the help we can get if we're going to expose these guys."

Boo barked in agreement, his tail wagging.

"All right, then," Sabrina said, a smile tugging at her lips. "Let's regroup and figure out our next move. The culinary cartel won't know what hit them."

As they set off into the night, the book of secrets tucked safely under Sabrina's arm, a flicker of movement caught her eye. There, in the shadows of the library, a figure watched them, a knowing smirk on their face. Sabrina's heart skipped a beat, realizing that their encounter with the cartel was far from over.

The bell above the door jingled as Sabrina and her team entered the Crossroads Diner, the familiar scent of coffee and spectral energy enveloping them like a comforting blanket. Sabrina led the way to the back room, where they often gathered to discuss matters of the paranormal and culinary.

"All right, team," Sabrina said, "It's time to get down to business. We need to gather more evidence against the culinary cartel.

Mort, his skeletal frame draped in his signature black robes, leaned against the wall, his scythe propped beside him. "I'll reach out to my contacts in the afterlife. They've got a knack for uncovering secrets, even from the most tight-lipped spirits."

Pepper grinned mischievously. "Leave the potion-making to me. I've got a recipe that'll enhance our senses and make us sharper than a chef's knife."

Boo, the resident ghost dog, barked in agreement, his ethereal tail wagging with excitement. Sabrina couldn't help but smile at her loyal companion, knowing that his keen nose could sniff out even the most elusive paranormal clues.

As the team set to work, Sabrina closed her eyes, reaching out to the ghostly patrons of the diner. "If anyone has information on the culinary cartel," she whispered, her voice echoing through the spectral plane, "please, come forward. We need your help."

The room grew still, the only sound the bubbling of Pepper's potion and the occasional creak of Mort's bones. Suddenly, a chill ran down Sabrina's spine, and she opened her eyes to find a ghostly figure materializing before her.

"Beware," the spirit whispered, its voice like the rustling of dry leaves. "There is a traitor among you. Trust no one."

Sabrina's heart raced, and she exchanged a worried glance with Mort. The grim reaper's eye sockets glowed with an eerie light, his expression grim. "A traitor?" he murmured, his voice low and foreboding. "But who?"

Pepper, her brow furrowed in concentration, looked up from her potion. "I could cast a truth-revealing spell," she suggested, her voice laced with determination. "It might help us identify the traitor."

Sabrina nodded, her mind racing with possibilities. Who among them could be working against their cause? She trusted her team implicitly, but the ghostly warning had planted a seed of doubt in her mind.

As Pepper began to prepare the spell, Sabrina paced the room. Boo followed at her heels, his ghostly presence a comforting constant in the midst of the uncertainty.

The room crackled with magical energy as Pepper chanted the incantation, her tattoos glowing with an otherworldly light. Sabrina held her breath, her heart pounding in her chest as she waited for the spell to take effect.

But just as the truth was about to be revealed, a sudden gust of wind swept through the room, extinguishing the candles and plunging them into darkness. Sabrina gasped, her senses on high alert as she reached for Mort's bony hand.

"What's happening?" she whispered, her voice trembling with fear.

A sinister laugh echoed through the darkness, sending shivers down Sabrina's spine. "You'll never uncover the truth," a disembodied voice taunted. "The culinary cartel will prevail, and you'll all be nothing more than ghosts in the wind."

With a final gust of wind, the room fell silent, leaving Sabrina and her team in the dark, their hearts racing with the realization that the stakes had just been raised. The traitor, it seemed, was closer than they ever imagined.

Sabrina blinked as her eyes adjusted to the sudden darkness, the sinister laughter still ringing in her ears. "Is everyone okay?" she asked, her voice wavering slightly.

Mort's bony hand squeezed hers reassuringly. "I'm fine, but I can't say the same for my pride. That voice really knew how to hit where it hurts."

Pepper's tattoos pulsed with a faint glow, casting an eerie light. "I'm not giving up that easily. We've come too far to let some disembodied voice scare us off."

Boo whimpered, his ghostly form flickering in and out of view. Sabrina reached out to comfort him, her hand passing through his ethereal fur. "It's okay, Boo. We'll get to the bottom of this."

Who could the traitor be? And how did they manage to infiltrate their tight-knit group?

Mort's voice cut through her thoughts. "I say we continue with the truth-revealing spell. It's our best chance at getting some answers."

Sabrina nodded, her resolve strengthening. "You're right. We can't let fear hold us back. Pepper, are you ready?"

The witch cracked her knuckles, a mischievous grin spreading across her face. "Born ready. Let's do this."

As Pepper began to weave the spell once more, Sabrina couldn't shake the feeling that they were being watched. The air seemed to crackle with an unseen energy, and she swore she could feel the weight of someone's gaze on the back of her neck.

Just as the spell reached its crescendo, a blinding light filled the room, causing everyone to shield their eyes. When the light faded, a glowing orb hovered in the center of the room, pulsing with an otherworldly energy.

"The truth lies within," Pepper whispered, her eyes wide with awe.

Sabrina stepped forward, her hand trembling as she reached out to touch the orb. As her fingers brushed its surface, a jolt of energy coursed through her body, and she gasped as a vision filled her mind.

In the vision, she saw Boo, his ghostly form flickering as he paced back and forth in front of a shadowy figure. The figure leaned forward, whispering something in Boo's ear, and the ghost dog's tail drooped in defeat.

Sabrina pulled her hand back, her heart racing as she turned to face her team. "I saw Boo," she said, her voice shaking. "He was talking to someone, someone from the culinary cartel."

Boo whimpered, his eyes downcast as the team turned to stare at him in disbelief. Sabrina shook her head, refusing to believe what she had seen.

"There has to be an explanation," she said, her voice filled with determination. "Boo would never betray us. Not willingly, at least."

Mort nodded, his skeletal face creased in thought. "Perhaps he's being coerced. Or maybe there's more to this vision than meets the eye."

Pepper's tattoos glowed with a fierce intensity. "Only one way to find out. We need to confront Boo and get the truth, once and for all."

As the team turned to face their ghostly companion, Boo's form flickered and faded, his soulful eyes filled with a mix of fear and resignation. The truth, it seemed, was more complex than any of them had imagined, and uncovering it would test the bonds of their friendship like never before.

The team split up, each determined to uncover the truth behind the unsettling vision. Sabrina and Mort headed to the library's paranormal section, hoping to find answers in the ancient tomes and scrolls. The musty smell of old books filled their nostrils as they pored over the yellowed pages, searching for any mention of truth-revealing spells gone awry.

"I don't understand," Sabrina muttered, her brow furrowed in concentration. "The spell should have been foolproof. How could it have implicated Boo?"

Spectres and Souffles

Mort ran a bony finger along the spine of a particularly old book, his voice laced with dark humor. "In my experience, nothing is ever truly foolproof. There's always a loophole, a hidden catch that can turn even the most well-intentioned magic on its head."

Meanwhile, Pepper and Boo set out to investigate the ghost dog's movements over the past few days. Pepper's tattoos glowed with a soft, pulsing light as she cast a tracking spell, following Boo's ethereal footprints through the streets of the town.

"I don't believe for a second that you betrayed us," Pepper said, her voice filled with fierce loyalty. "We'll get to the bottom of this, Boo. I promise."

Boo whimpered softly, his translucent tail wagging in appreciation as they made their way towards the outskirts of town. As they approached an abandoned warehouse, Pepper's tattoos flared with a sudden intensity, and Boo let out a low, warning growl.

"Someone's in there," Pepper whispered, her eyes narrowing as she peered into the darkness. "And I don't think they're friendly."

Inside the warehouse, Sabrina and Mort arrived, having followed a cryptic clue from one of the ancient texts. The air was thick with the tang of dark magic, and the shadows seemed to writhe with a malevolent presence.

"Sabrina, Mort, watch out!" Pepper cried, her voice ringing through the cavernous space.

But it was too late. A blast of searing energy erupted from the shadows, engulfing the team in a blinding light. When the smoke cleared, they found themselves face to face with a hooded figure, his eyes glinting with malice.

"You should have left well enough alone," the figure hissed, his voice dripping with venom. "Now, you'll pay the price for your meddling."

As the figure raised his hands, preparing to unleash another devastating spell, Boo leapt forward, his ghostly form shimmering with an unearthly light. The ghost dog stood between his friends and the hooded figure, his stance defiant and unyielding.

The figure laughed, a cold, cruel sound that echoed through the warehouse. "You think you can protect them, dog? You, who have already betrayed them once?"

Boo growled as he prepared to face the unknown adversary. The team stood behind him, united in their resolve to uncover the truth and protect one another.

The hooded figure's laughter reverberated through the warehouse, sending chills down Sabrina's spine. She glanced at Mort, whose usually stoic expression had been replaced by one of grim determination. Pepper's hands crackled with magical energy, ready to defend her friends at a moment's notice.

"You've got it all wrong," Sabrina said, her voice steady despite the fear coursing through her veins. "Boo would never betray us. There's more to this than meets the eye."

The figure sneered, his eyes glinting beneath the shadows of his hood. "Is that so? Then why don't we put your little pet to the test?"

With a flick of his wrist, the figure sent a pulse of dark energy hurtling towards Boo. The ghost dog yelped in pain, his ethereal form flickering as the spell struck him.

"No!" Pepper cried, unleashing a burst of protective magic that shielded Boo from further harm. "Leave him alone, you monster!"

The figure's gaze shifted to Pepper, a cruel smile playing at the corners of his lips. "Ah, the witch. I've heard of your family's legacy. It's a shame you've chosen to waste your talents on these fools."

Mort stepped forward, his scythe materializing in his hand. "Enough talk. It's time to end this."

The figure laughed once more, the sound grating against their ears like nails on a chalkboard. "You have no idea what you're up against. But by all means, let's dance."

With those words, the warehouse erupted into chaos. Spells flew through the air, colliding with the walls and sending showers of sparks raining down upon them. Sabrina ducked and weaved, her heart pounding in her chest as she tried to stay one step ahead of the figure's attacks.

Spectres and Souffles

Boo, despite his injury, leapt into the fray, his ghostly jaws snapping at the figure's heels. Mort's scythe sliced through the air, barely missing the figure as he twisted away at the last moment.

Pepper's magic surged through the room, a dazzling display of light and color that momentarily blinded their adversary. Taking advantage of the distraction, Sabrina lunged forward, her hands outstretched as she tried to unmask the figure.

But just as her fingers brushed against the rough fabric of the hood, the figure vanished in a swirl of inky darkness. The team stood, panting and bruised, staring at the empty space where their enemy had stood just moments before.

"Is everyone okay?" Sabrina asked, her voice trembling slightly as the adrenaline began to fade.

Mort nodded, his scythe disappearing as he surveyed the damage. "We'll live. But we need answers, and fast."

Pepper knelt beside Boo, her hands glowing with healing magic as she tended to his wounds. "I don't understand. Why would anyone want to frame Boo?"

Sabrina shook her head, her mind racing with possibilities. "I don't know. But one thing's for sure - we're not going to rest until we get to the bottom of this."

As the team regrouped, their resolve stronger than ever, the scent of singed fabric and the tang of magical residue hung heavy in the air. The warehouse creaked and groaned around them, as if whispering secrets they had yet to uncover.

Chapter 11

The kitchen of the Crossroads Diner hummed with nervous energy as Sabrina and her eclectic team huddled around the stainless steel prep table.

"François has gone too far this time," she declared. "We can't let his supernatural shenanigans ruin our customers' dining experience!"

Mort, the skeletal line cook, nodded gravely, his bony fingers tapping against the metal table. "I've seen some strange things in my afterlife, but François's creations take the cake - literally."

Pepper, rolled her eyes. "That man's ego is bigger than his chef's hat. We need to put a stop to his meddling before he scares away all our regulars - both living and dead."

Boo, Sabrina's faithful ghost dog, let out a concerned whine, his translucent tail thumping anxiously against the tiled floor. Sabrina reached down to give him a comforting scratch behind the ears.

"Don't worry, Boo. François may have some fancy culinary tricks up his sleeve, but we've got the power of teamwork and a pinch of paranormal mojo on our side."

Just then, a blood-curdling scream pierced the air, causing the team to exchange alarmed glances. They rushed out of the kitchen and into the dining area, where they were greeted by a sight that made even Mort's jaw drop.

There, towering over the terrified patrons, stood a colossal dessert that defied both culinary norms and the laws of physics. The monstrosity oozed an otherworldly, neon-green glow, its gelatinous layers undulating menacingly. A sinister aroma wafted from its core, a sickly-sweet blend of cotton candy and decay that made Sabrina's stomach churn.

"What in the name of all things sugary is that?" Pepper gasped.

Spectres and Souffles

Sabrina's mind raced as she took in the scene, her heart pounding against her ribcage. This was no ordinary dessert - it was a paranormal pastry nightmare come to life, and it was up to her and her team to stop it before it wreaked havoc on the unsuspecting diners.

As the towering confection let out an unearthly roar, Sabrina steeled herself. She knew that François's supernatural culinary creations were growing more powerful by the day.

Sabrina stepped forward, her eyes locked on the menacing dessert. "Alright," she called out, her voice steady despite the chaos around her. "It's time to put this sweet nightmare to bed!"

Mort chuckled darkly, his skeletal fingers tightening around the handle of his scythe at the ready. "I never thought I'd say this, but I'm ready to reap some dessert."

As the towering confection lashed out with a gelatinous tendril, Sabrina closed her eyes and focused her energy on communicating with the spirit within the creation. "Listen to me," she whispered, her voice echoing through the ethereal plane. "You don't have to do this. We can help you find peace."

The spirit's response was a garbled mix of anguish and rage, its words dripping with the same sickly-sweet aroma that emanated from the dessert. Sabrina's heart ached for the tormented soul, but she knew she had to act fast to protect the innocent diners.

Mort leaped into action, his scythe slicing through the air as he fended off the dessert's attacks. The blade hummed with an otherworldly energy, leaving trails of sparkling mist in its wake. "I've got your back, Sabrina!"

Pepper, not one to be left out of the fray, summoned her magic and cast a spell to create a gust of wind. "Take this, you overgrown pastry!" she shouted, her fiery hair whipping around her face as the wind whirled through the diner.

But the dessert was not so easily subdued. As the gust of wind hit its gelatinous form, it suddenly multiplied, splitting into a dozen smaller, equally dangerous versions of itself. The mini-desserts scurried across the floor, leaving trails of sticky, glowing residue in their wake.

"Oh, for the love of—" Mort grumbled, his scythe now a blur as he tried to keep the multiplying menaces at bay.

Sabrina's mind raced as she watched the chaos unfold. She knew they needed a plan, and fast. The spirit within the dessert was growing more agitated by the second, and she could feel its anguish threatening to overwhelm her senses.

She took a deep breath, the sweet and sour tang of the diner's signature dishes mingling with the acrid scent of fear and uncertainty.

As the mini-desserts closed in, their gelatinous forms pulsing with an eerie, otherworldly light, Sabrina steeled herself for the next phase of the fight. She glanced at Mort and Pepper, a silent understanding passing between them.

But first, they had to survive the onslaught of the multiplying, menacing desserts that threatened to engulf them all in a wave of supernatural sweetness gone sour.

"Mort, keep those desserts away from us!" Sabrina shouted over the commotion. "Pepper and I need time to cast a spell that will neutralize their supernatural properties."

Mort grunted in acknowledgment, his scythe slicing through the air with renewed vigor. "You got it, boss. Just hurry up, will you? These little buggers are getting on my last nerve."

Sabrina turned to Pepper, "Pep, remember that spell we used last week to stop that rogue soufflé from terrorizing the kitchen?"

Pepper's face lit up, her wild red curls bouncing as she nodded enthusiastically. "The one that made it deflate like a sad balloon? Absolutely!"

"I think it's time for an encore performance," Sabrina grinned, extending her hand to Pepper.

The two women joined hands, their fingers intertwining as they began to chant in unison. The air around them crackled with energy, the scent of cinnamon and sage swirling together in a heady mix.

As the spell took hold, the mini-desserts began to shudder and convulse, their once-vibrant colors fading to a dull, lifeless gray. One by one, they collapsed in on themselves, reduced to nothing more than piles of inert goo.

Mort lowered his scythe, a wry smile tugging at the corners of his skeletal mouth. "Well, that was a sticky situation if I ever saw one."

Spectres and Souffles

Sabrina and Pepper exchanged a look, their laughter ringing out through the diner as the tension of the moment dissolved. But their relief was short-lived as they surveyed the aftermath of the supernatural skirmish.

"This is getting out of hand," Sabrina sighed, her brow furrowing with concern. "François's creations are becoming more powerful and unpredictable by the day. We need to find a way to stop him before he puts the entire diner and its customers at risk."

Pepper nodded, her expression uncharacteristically serious. "Agreed. But how do we even begin to tackle a problem like this? It's not like we can just waltz into his kitchen and ask him to knock it off."

Mort chuckled darkly, his eye sockets glowing with a mischievous light. "Maybe not, but I bet we could give him a taste of his own medicine. Fight fire with fire, or in this case, magic with magic."

Sabrina considered his words, a plan already forming in her mind. She knew that they couldn't afford to underestimate François, but she also knew that with her team's unique abilities and unwavering determination, they had a fighting chance.

As the sun began to set outside the diner's windows, casting long shadows across the checkered floor, Sabrina squared her shoulders and turned to face her friends. "Alright, team. Let's regroup and figure out our next move. Failure is not on the menu."

A sudden commotion from the kitchen jolted Sabrina out of her thoughts. The clattering of pots and pans mingled with the hiss of boiling water, creating a discordant symphony that set her nerves on edge. She exchanged a wary glance with Mort and Pepper before cautiously making her way towards the sound, her heart pounding in her chest.

As they pushed through the swinging doors, the trio found themselves face to face with a nightmarish scene. A massive, writhing creature towered over them, its form a grotesque amalgamation of various savory dishes. Razor-sharp claws made of twisted cutlery glinted menacingly in the fluorescent light, while a gaping maw lined with jagged shards of porcelain plates snapped hungrily in their direction.

"Well, that's a sight for sore eye sockets," Mort quipped, his scythe materializing in his bony hands. "Looks like François has been playing with his food again."

Sabrina swallowed hard, her mind racing as she tried to make sense of the monstrosity before them. She could sense the tormented spirits that had been woven into the creature's essence, their anguished cries echoing in her mind. "We need to contain it before it reaches the customers," she said, her voice tight with urgency.

Pepper nodded, her hands already crackling with arcane energy. "I've got an idea. Mort, keep that thing busy while Sabrina and I work on a barrier spell."

The grim reaper grinned, his eye sockets flashing with anticipation. "With pleasure, Pep. I've been itching for a good fight all day."

As Mort charged forward, his scythe slicing through the air, Sabrina focused her attention on the trapped spirits within the creature. She reached out with her mind, her voice a soothing balm amidst the chaos. "I know you're in pain," she whispered, "but we're here to help. Please, lend me your strength so we can end this madness."

The spirits responded to her call, their essence intertwining with her own in a brilliant dance of light and shadow. Sabrina felt their power coursing through her veins, a dizzying rush of energy that threatened to overwhelm her senses.

Beside her, Pepper chanted in an ancient tongue, her words weaving a tapestry of protective magic around the perimeter of the kitchen. Tendrils of flame sprang from her fingertips, forming a shimmering barrier that pulsed with an otherworldly glow.

The creature let out a deafening roar, its claws scrabbling against the magical flames as it sought to break through. Mort danced around its flailing limbs, his scythe a blur of motion as he struck again and again, his laughter ringing out above the din.

Sabrina gritted her teeth, the strain of maintaining her connection with the spirits taking its toll. She could feel their pain, their desperation, and knew that she had to act fast. With a final surge of energy, she channeled the spirits' power into the barrier, reinforcing it with a blinding flash of light.

The creature recoiled, its form shuddering and shrinking as the spirits were pulled free from its grasp. It let out a final, agonized shriek before collapsing into a heap of shattered dishes and congealed sauces, its once-terrifying visage reduced to nothing more than a culinary disaster.

Sabrina sagged against the counter, her breath coming in ragged gasps. Mort and Pepper were at her side in an instant, their faces etched with concern.

"You okay, boss?" Mort asked, his usually sardonic tone softened by worry.

Sabrina managed a weak smile, "I will be," she said, "but we can't rest yet. François is still out there, and who knows what other twisted creations he has in store for us."

Boo's frantic barking jolted Sabrina from her momentary respite, his ghostly form darting around the monstrous creature's legs in a desperate attempt to draw its attention. The savory beast snarled, its razor-sharp claws slashing through the air as it tried to strike the spectral canine.

"Good boy, Boo!" Sabrina called out, her voice strained with exhaustion. "Keep it distracted!"

Seizing the opportunity, Sabrina closed her eyes and focused her energy on the spirit within the creature. The din of the kitchen faded away as she delved deeper into the ethereal realm, searching for the thread that bound the spirit to its culinary prison.

"Come on, come on," she muttered under her breath, her brow furrowed in concentration. "Where are you hiding?"

As if in response, a faint whisper echoed through her mind, a distant cry for help amidst the chaos. Sabrina's eyes snapped open, a triumphant grin spreading across her face.

"Garlic!" she exclaimed, her voice cutting through the cacophony of the kitchen. "The creature's weakness is garlic!"

Mort and Pepper exchanged a skeptical glance, their eyebrows raised in disbelief.

"Garlic?" Mort scoffed, his scythe still poised to strike. "What is this, a bad vampire movie?"

Pepper, however, was already rummaging through the pantry, her hands a blur as she searched for the pungent bulbs. "Found them!" she cried, tossing a handful of garlic cloves to Sabrina.

Without hesitation, Sabrina began to chant, her voice low and melodic as she wove the ancient words of power. The garlic cloves in her hand began to glow with an ethereal light, pulsing in time with the rhythm of her incantation.

Mort, seeing his chance, lunged forward, his scythe slicing through the air with deadly precision. The blade struck the creature's spirit, severing its connection to the mortal realm with a blinding flash of light.

The creature let out a deafening roar, its form shuddering and convulsing as the garlic's power coursed through its being. Slowly, painfully, it began to shrink, its monstrous visage melting away to reveal the harmless dish beneath.

Sabrina sagged against the counter, her energy spent. Boo, sensing her exhaustion, padded over and nuzzled her hand, his ghostly fur cool and comforting against her skin.

"Good work, team," she said, a tired smile playing at the corners of her mouth.

The sun had long since set, and the Crossroads Diner was bathed in the warm glow of the vintage neon signs that adorned its walls. Sabrina and her team had spent hours cleaning up the remnants of their battles, scrubbing ectoplasmic goo from the floors and wiping the last traces of enchanted seasoning from the countertops.

"I don't know about you guys," Pepper said, her voice tinged with exhaustion, "but I could really go for a midnight snack right about now."

Mort chuckled darkly, his skeletal face contorting into a wry grin. "After everything we've seen today, I'm not sure I'll ever look at food the same way again."

Sabrina opened her mouth to respond, but before she could utter a word, the ground beneath their feet began to tremble. The walls of the diner shook, and the lights flickered ominously overhead.

"What in the name of all that's holy..." Sabrina muttered, her eyes widening in disbelief as a massive, writhing form began to take shape in the center of the kitchen.

It was a colossal main course, towering over them like a mountain of meat and vegetables. Its surface pulsed with an otherworldly energy, and the air around it crackled with malevolent power.

"François," Sabrina whispered, her voice barely audible over the deafening roar of the creature's aura. "He's really outdone himself this time."

Pepper and Mort instinctively moved to flank Sabrina. Boo growled low in his throat, his ghostly hackles rising as he sensed the danger that loomed before them.

"Alright, team," Sabrina said, her voice steady despite the fear that gripped her heart. "This is it. The battle we've been preparing for. We can't let François win, no matter what."

She reached out to take Pepper's hand, feeling the warmth of her friend's skin against her own. Mort placed a bony hand on her shoulder, his touch oddly reassuring in the face of such overwhelming odds.

Together, they braced themselves for the fight of their afterlives.

The monstrous main course loomed over the team, its aroma a nauseating blend of savory and sinister. Tendrils of steam curled from its surface, carrying with them the faint whispers of tormented souls.

"I don't suppose anyone has a giant fork?" Mort quipped, his skeletal grin stretching wide.

Pepper rolled her eyes. "Not helpful, Mort. We need a plan, and fast."

Sabrina's mind raced, searching for a solution. She reached out with her spirit-sensing abilities, trying to understand the nature of the beast before them. A cacophony of voices assaulted her mind, each one crying out in agony and despair.

"It's not just one spirit," she gasped, clutching her head. "It's dozens, maybe hundreds. All trapped within this twisted creation."

The creature shuddered, as if sensing Sabrina's intrusion. With a roar that shook the very foundations of the diner, it lashed out, sending a wave of searing heat and razor-sharp utensils flying toward the team.

Mort reacted instantly, his scythe a blur of motion as he deflected the incoming projectiles. Pepper conjured a shimmering shield of energy, protecting Sabrina and Boo from the onslaught.

"We can't let it escape the kitchen!" Sabrina shouted over the chaos. "If it gets out into the diner, our customers will be in danger!"

Boo barked in agreement, his ghostly form phasing through the countertops as he charged toward the creature, intent on distracting it.

Sabrina and Pepper exchanged a determined glance, their hands clasping together as they began to chant in unison. The air around them crackled with power, a swirling vortex of spiritual energy that grew with each passing second.

But even as they poured their combined strength into the spell, the creature seemed to absorb the energy, growing larger and more menacing with every moment. Its form shifted and twisted, taking on the nightmarish aspects of the spirits trapped within.

François's laughter echoed through the kitchen, a mocking reminder of the challenge they faced. Sabrina gritted her teeth, her resolve hardening in the face of his taunts.

They would find a way to stop this culinary abomination, to free the spirits trapped within and put an end to François's meddling once and for all. But as the creature reared up, its maw gaping wide to unleash another devastating attack, Sabrina couldn't help but wonder if they were already too late...

Chapter 12

Sunlight streamed through the dusty blinds of Sabrina's office, casting a golden glow on the chaotic mess before her. Stacks of papers and photographs littered every surface, a testament to the mystery she was determined to unravel. With a deep breath, Sabrina rolled up the sleeves of her dress and dove headfirst into the evidence.

She sifted through the papers, her brow furrowed in concentration as she attempted to piece together the events leading up to François's untimely demise. The clues were scattered, like breadcrumbs leading to a gingerbread house of secrets. Sabrina's mind raced as she connected the dots, creating a timeline that would make any detective proud.

Amidst the sea of information, a memory surfaced—a conversation with Eliot just days ago. His words echoed in her mind, a tantalizing hint of something amiss. "I had a strange encounter with François that night," he had said, his eyes clouded with an emotion Sabrina couldn't quite decipher.

She tapped her pen against her lips, lost in thought. What could Eliot know about François's death? The dishwasher was as mysterious as a locked diary, his secrets guarded by a cover of suds and steam. Sabrina's curiosity burned brighter than a ghost pepper, and she knew she had to confront him.

With a determined nod, Sabrina gathered the most pertinent documents and marched out of her office, her vintage heels clicking against the checkered floor. The diner buzzed with the chatter of patrons, both living and deceased, but Sabrina's focus was solely on the kitchen.

She pushed through the swinging doors, the smell of freshly baked apple pie enveloping her like a warm hug. Eliot stood at the sink, his hands submerged in soapy water as he meticulously scrubbed a pot. Sabrina approached him, her voice as sweet as the pie filling.

"Eliot, do you have a moment? I need to talk to you about something important."

The dishwasher glanced up before returning to the task at hand. "Sure, boss. What's on your mind?"

Sabrina leaned against the counter, her fingers tracing the edge of a photograph. "I was going through the evidence related to François's death, and I remembered you mentioning a strange encounter with him that night. Can you tell me more about it?"

Eliot's hands stilled in the water, suds dripping from his fingertips. The air in the kitchen grew thick with tension, like a roux on the verge of burning. Slowly, he turned to face Sabrina, his expression as unreadable as a menu written in hieroglyphics.

"I'm not sure what you're getting at, Sabrina. It was just a brief run-in, nothing more."

But Sabrina wasn't buying it. She could sense the secrets simmering beneath Eliot's cool exterior, like a pot ready to boil over. She leaned in closer, her voice barely above a whisper.

"Eliot, if you know something—anything—about what happened to François, you need to tell me. We're all in this together, and the truth needs to come out."

The dishwasher's jaw clenched, his gaze flickering between Sabrina and the stack of dirty dishes. The seconds ticked by, each one as heavy as a cast-iron skillet. Finally, Eliot let out a sigh, his shoulders sagging under the weight of his secrets.

"Alright, Sabrina. I'll tell you what I know, but you might not like what you hear..."

The kitchen fell silent, the only sound the gentle hum of the refrigerator. Sabrina held her breath, her heart pounding in her chest like a meat tenderizer. She knew she was on the precipice of a breakthrough, but the question remained—what dark truths lay hidden beneath the suds?

Sabrina leaned against the stainless steel countertop, her fingers drumming a staccato rhythm as she waited for Eliot to continue. The dishwasher wiped his hands on his apron, leaving behind damp handprints that resembled Rorschach tests.

Spectres and Souffles

"It's true, I did see François that night," Eliot admitted, his voice barely audible over the clatter of dishes. "He was agitated, rambling on about some big secret he'd uncovered. I tried to calm him down, but he was adamant about exposing the truth."

Sabrina's eyebrows shot up, her curiosity piqued. "What kind of secret? Did he give you any details?"

Eliot shook his head, his gaze fixed on the floor. "No, he was too worked up to make much sense. But he kept mentioning something about a 'culinary conspiracy' and how he had proof that could bring down some powerful people."

The pieces of the puzzle began to fall into place in Sabrina's mind, like ingredients coming together in a recipe. She knew François had been investigating the celebrity chef world, but the scope of his findings had remained a mystery.

"Eliot, this is crucial information. Why didn't you come forward sooner?" Sabrina asked, her tone gentle but firm.

The dishwasher's shoulders tensed, his fingers gripping the edge of the sink. "I... I was afraid. François made me swear not to tell anyone, said it was too dangerous. I thought I was protecting him by keeping quiet."

Sabrina placed a comforting hand on Eliot's arm, feeling the warmth of his skin through his damp sleeve. "I understand, but we're in this together now. We need to find out what François discovered and why it got him killed."

Eliot nodded, a flicker of determination in his eyes. "I want to help, Sabrina. François was my friend, and I owe it to him to see this through."

As the two stood in the kitchen, surrounded by the clatter of dishes and the hiss of the faucet, Sabrina felt a surge of hope.

But even as they forged this newfound alliance, Sabrina couldn't shake the feeling that they were being watched. The shadows seemed to lengthen, the air growing thick with an unseen presence. She shivered, wondering if the spirits of the diner were trying to tell her something... or if something far more sinister was lurking just out of sight.

Sabrina's mind raced as she processed Eliot's revelation. François had discovered something about the celebrity chef cartel, and it had cost him his life. The pieces of the puzzle were starting to fall into place, but there were still so many unanswered questions.

She looked at Eliot, searching his face for any hint of deception. "Eliot, I need you to be completely honest with me. Did you have any idea what François was planning to do with this information?"

Eliot shifted uncomfortably, his gaze darting around the kitchen as if seeking an escape route. "I... I didn't know the specifics. François was always secretive about his investigations. But I could tell he was onto something big, something that scared him."

Sabrina's heart quickened, a sense of urgency building within her. "We need to find out what he knew, Eliot. It could be the key to solving this whole mystery."

Eliot rubbed his chin thoughtfully, the stubble rasping against his fingers. "There might be a way. François had a hidden safe in his apartment where he kept all his sensitive information. If we could get our hands on those files..."

Sabrina's eyes widened with realization. "That's it! We need to go to François's apartment and find that safe. But we can't go charging in there without a plan. The cartel might be watching, waiting for someone to make a move."

Eliot nodded, a grim determination settling over his features. "You're right. We need to be smart about this. I can scope out the apartment, see if there's any suspicious activity. Then we can come up with a plan to get inside undetected."

As they plotted their next move, Sabrina couldn't help but feel a growing sense of unease. She had always believed in the power of the paranormal, but this was different. The stakes were higher, the dangers more tangible. She couldn't shake the feeling that they were being watched, that the cartel had eyes and ears everywhere.

The sun had long since set by the time Sabrina and Eliot left the diner, casting long shadows across the quiet streets. The air was thick with tension, a palpable sense of anticipation that set Sabrina's nerves on edge. She glanced over at Eliot as they walked briskly towards François's apartment.

"Are you sure about this?" Sabrina asked, her voice barely above a whisper. "We don't know what we're walking into."

Eliot's jaw clenched, his eyes scanning the shadows for any sign of movement. "We don't have a choice. If we don't act now, the cartel will just keep getting away with murder. Literally."

Sabrina nodded, a shiver running down her spine. She knew he was right, but the thought of confronting the cartel head-on was terrifying. She had always relied on her otherworldly abilities to guide her, but now she felt like she was flying blind.

As they approached the apartment building, Eliot held up a hand, signaling for Sabrina to stop. He peered around the corner, his eyes narrowing as he surveyed the scene.

"There's a light on in François's apartment," he murmured, his voice low and urgent. "Someone's inside."

Sabrina's heart raced, her palms slick with sweat. "What do we do?"

Eliot turned to face her, his expression grim. "We go in. But we have to be careful. They could be armed."

Sabrina swallowed hard. She had never been in a situation like this before, and the thought of walking into danger made her stomach churn.

With a deep breath, she nodded.

Eliot led the way, his movements swift and silent as they crept up the stairs. Sabrina followed close behind, her senses on high alert. She could feel the presence of spirits all around her, their whispers a haunting chorus in her ears.

As they reached François's door, Eliot paused, his hand hovering over the handle. He glanced back at Sabrina, a silent question in his eyes. She nodded, her heart pounding in her chest.

With a deep breath, Eliot turned the handle, the door swinging open with a soft creak. The apartment was dark, the only light coming from a single lamp in the corner. Sabrina squinted, trying to make out the shapes in the shadows.

Suddenly, a figure stepped out from behind the door, a gun pointed directly at Eliot's head. Sabrina gasped, her blood turning to ice in her veins.

"Well, well, well," a familiar voice drawled, sending a chill down Sabrina's spine. "Look what the cat dragged in."

Sabrina's eyes widened in recognition, her heart skipping a beat. She knew that voice, knew it all too well. It was a voice she had hoped never to hear again, a voice that haunted her dreams and made her blood run cold.

The figure stepped into the light, a smirk playing across his lips. It was none other than Chef Ricardo Moretti, the mastermind behind the celebrity chef cartel. And he had them right where he wanted them.

Sabrina's heart raced as she stared at the barrel of the gun, her mind frantically searching for a way out of this deadly situation. Eliot remained still, his eyes locked on Chef Moretti.

"I always knew you were a liability, Eliot," Moretti sneered, his voice dripping with disdain. "But teaming up with this meddlesome diner owner? That's a new low, even for you."

Eliot's jaw clenched, his hands balling into fists at his sides. "You've gone too far, Moretti. It's time for the truth to come out."

Moretti let out a harsh laugh, the sound echoing in the dimly lit apartment. "The truth? You think anyone cares about the truth in this industry? It's all about power, my dear boy. And I have it all."

Sabrina's mind raced, desperately trying to find a way to diffuse the situation. She took a tentative step forward, her voice trembling slightly as she spoke. "Chef Moretti, please. Violence isn't the answer. We can find a way to resolve this peacefully."

Moretti's gaze shifted to Sabrina, his eyes narrowing. "Ah, the voice of reason. How quaint. But I'm afraid it's far too late for peace, my dear. You've stuck your nose where it doesn't belong, and now you'll pay the price."

Eliot tensed, his body coiled like a spring ready to launch. Sabrina could see the wheels turning in his head, calculating the risks and weighing their options. She knew they had to act fast, or they'd both end up as ghosts in her diner.

Suddenly, a loud crash sounded from the kitchen, startling everyone in the room. Moretti's head whipped around, his gun momentarily lowering. Seizing the opportunity, Eliot lunged forward, tackling Moretti to the ground. The gun clattered to the floor, sliding across the hardwood.

Spectres and Souffles

Sabrina dove for the weapon, her fingers closing around the cool metal. She pointed it at Moretti, her hands shaking. "It's over, Chef. The authorities are on their way. You're finished."

Moretti's face contorted with rage, his eyes blazing. "You think this is the end? You have no idea what you've started. The cartel is bigger than you can imagine. You'll never be safe, not as long as I'm alive."

As if on cue, sirens wailed in the distance, growing louder with each passing second. Sabrina and Eliot exchanged a glance, a flicker of hope igniting in their hearts. Help was on the way.

But Moretti had one last trick up his sleeve. With a swift motion, he reached into his pocket and pulled out a small device. Sabrina's eyes widened in horror as she realized what it was: a detonator.

"If I can't have my empire," Moretti snarled, his thumb hovering over the button, "then no one can. Say goodbye to your precious diner, Sabrina. It's about to become a pile of rubble."

Sabrina's heart stopped, her world tilting on its axis. The Crossroads Diner, her sanctuary, her home, was in danger. And she was powerless to stop it.

The sirens grew deafening as the authorities approached, but Sabrina barely heard them. All she could focus on was the malevolent gleam in Moretti's eyes and the weight of the gun in her hand.

The scene froze, suspended in a moment of heart-stopping tension. The fate of the Crossroads Diner, and the lives of everyone inside, hung in the balance. Sabrina and Eliot's unlikely alliance had led them to this precipice, but would it be enough to save them from the looming destruction?

Sabrina's mind raced, trying to find a way out of this dangerous situation. She glanced at Eliot, who stood rigid beside her, his eyes locked on Moretti's gun. The air in the kitchen felt heavy, the silence broken only by the humming of the refrigerator and the distant clatter of dishes from the diner.

"Moretti," Sabrina said, her voice steady despite the fear coursing through her veins. "You don't have to do this. We can talk this through, find a peaceful solution."

Moretti let out a harsh laugh, the sound grating against Sabrina's ears. "Peaceful solution? You've been sticking your nose where it doesn't belong, and now you think you can negotiate with me?"

Eliot stepped forward, his hands raised in a placating gesture. "Luciano, please. We were friends once, remember? We all wanted the same thing - to create something beautiful, to share our passion with the world."

Moretti's grip on the gun tightened, his knuckles turning white. "Friends? You betrayed me, Eliot. You and François, plotting behind my back, trying to destroy everything I've built."

Sabrina's heart ached for Eliot, seeing the pain and regret etched on his face. She knew that he had made mistakes, but she also believed in the goodness within him. If only Moretti could see it too.

"It's not too late," Sabrina said softly, her voice barely above a whisper. "You can still choose a different path, Luciano. One that doesn't end in violence and bloodshed."

For a moment, Moretti's eyes flickered with uncertainty, and Sabrina dared to hope that her words had reached him. But then his expression hardened, and he shook his head.

"No. It's too late for that. I've come too far to turn back now."

He raised the gun, aiming it directly at Sabrina's heart. She heard Eliot's sharp intake of breath beside her, felt the world slow down around her.

And then, just as Moretti's finger tightened on the trigger, the kitchen door burst open once more, and a figure rushed in, tackling Moretti to the ground.

Sabrina blinked, her mind struggling to process the sudden turn of events. She watched as the newcomer wrestled with Moretti, the gun clattering to the floor and skidding across the tiles.

It was only when the fight had ended, with Moretti subdued and the gun safely in the hands of the mysterious savior, that Sabrina realized who it was.

"François?" she gasped, her voice trembling with disbelief.

Spectres and Souffles

There, standing before them, was the ghostly form of François himself, looking exactly as he had in life. He smiled at Sabrina and Eliot, a twinkle in his eye.

"Did you really think I'd let you face this alone?" he said, his voice echoing with an otherworldly resonance.

As Sabrina and Eliot stared at him, their minds reeling with questions and emotions, they knew that their journey was far from over. But with François by their side, they felt a renewed sense of hope and determination.

Together, they would unravel the secrets of the celebrity chef cartel and bring justice to the culinary world, one dish at a time.

Sabrina's heart raced as she stared at the ghostly figure of François, her mind struggling to comprehend the reality of his presence. The adrenaline from the confrontation with Moretti still coursed through her veins, mixing with the overwhelming relief and confusion at seeing her departed friend once more.

"But... how?" she managed to whisper, her voice trembling with emotion.

François's translucent form shimmered in the fluorescent light of the kitchen as he approached Sabrina and Eliot, his footsteps making no sound on the tiled floor. The faint aroma of saffron and rosemary seemed to follow him, a ghostly reminder of his culinary prowess.

"Let's just say that even death couldn't keep me from protecting those I care about," François replied, his voice carrying a hint of mischief. "And from ensuring that the truth about the cartel is finally brought to light."

Eliot, still reeling from the revelation of François's ghostly presence, found his voice. "You knew about the cartel all along, didn't you? That's why they targeted you."

François nodded solemnly. "I had my suspicions, but I needed proof. And I knew that if anything happened to me, Sabrina would be the one to uncover the truth."

Sabrina felt a wave of emotions wash over her—gratitude, sorrow, and a renewed sense of purpose. She reached out instinctively, her hand passing through François's ethereal form, sending a shiver down her spine.

"François, I promise, I won't let you down," Sabrina vowed, her voice firm with determination. "We'll bring the cartel to light and ensure your legacy lives on."

A warm smile spread across François' ghostly face, his ethereal eyes shining with pride. "I never doubted you, Sabrina. But time is against us. The cartel's grip is strong, and they'll stop at nothing to protect their secrets."

The trio leaned in closer, their voices hushed with urgency as they began to hatch their plan. The cold, metallic surfaces of the kitchen seemed to hum with the tension and resolve in the air. Fragments of their conversation cut through the chill, as ideas clicked together like the pieces of a carefully laid puzzle.

"We'll need hard evidence," Eliot muttered, his brow furrowed in thought. "Something so undeniable, even the dirtiest officials can't sweep it under the rug."

Sabrina's eyes gleamed with mischief and determination. "I think I have just the thing," she said with a sly grin. "But it's going to take a little culinary magic—and a lot of luck."

Chapter 13

Sabrina's heart thundered in her chest as she stared at Eliot, her mind reeling. The dishwasher's form shimmered and distorted before her eyes, his lean frame expanding upward like rising dough. His dark hair lengthened and whipped in an unseen wind, and his blue eyes began to glow with an otherworldly light.

"Eliot, what...what's happening to you?" Sabrina stammered, taking an involuntary step back. The air around them crackled with energy, sending shivers down her spine.

Eliot's voice reverberated through the kitchen, deeper and more resonant than she had ever heard it. "Oh Sabrina, you have no idea who you're dealing with, do you?" He chuckled darkly as his transformation continued.

Pale skin hardened into scales that gleamed like polished obsidian. Fingernails elongated into razor-sharp talons. Eliot's face stretched and contorted, his nose and mouth fusing into a pointed snout filled with gleaming fangs. Sabrina's mind grasped for an explanation amidst the chaos. A demon? An ancient spirit? No, this was something else entirely...

Towering over her now, Eliot - or the creature he had become - flexed powerful limbs that ended in wickedly curved claws. Leathery wings unfurled from his back, their span nearly brushing the walls of the cramped kitchen. His eyes blazed with an inner fire, boring into Sabrina's very soul.

"I am Loki, god of mischief and trickery," he proclaimed, his voice echoing with centuries of power. "And you, my dear, have stumbled into a web far more tangled than you could possibly imagine."

Sabrina's mouth went dry. A trickster god? Working as a dishwasher in her diner? Her mind spun with the revelation, even as fear turned her blood to ice. What did an immortal being want with her humble establishment? And more urgently, what was she going to do now that she knew his true nature?

She swallowed hard, forcing herself to meet those glowing eyes. "Loki. I...I don't understand. Why are you here? What do you want?"

The god flashed a predatory grin, razor-sharp teeth glinting in the fluorescent light. "Oh, I want many things, Sabrina Spellworth. And you're going to help me get them."

Sabrina's shock turned to disbelief as Loki's words sank in. "Help you? Why would I help you? And what does any of this have to do with François's death?"

Loki's eyes narrowed, the glow dimming to a smoldering ember. "Everything," he hissed. "François was merely a pawn in a game that has been playing out for centuries. A game that the culinary world has been rigging against me for far too long."

He began to pace, his wings twitching with agitation. "You see, I have a bone to pick with chefs. They think themselves so clever, so innovative, but they are nothing more than thieves and charlatans. They steal the secrets of the gods and claim them as their own."

Sabrina frowned, trying to make sense of his words. "Secrets of the gods? What are you talking about?"

Loki whirled on her, his face contorted with ancient rage. "The secret to eternal life, hidden within the ambrosia of the gods. The power to control the minds of mortals, woven into the very spices they use. The ability to manipulate the elements, disguised as mere cooking techniques. Chefs have been stealing our magic for millennia, and I have had enough!"

He slammed his fist against the counter, sending pots and pans clattering to the floor. Sabrina flinched, her heart racing as she realized the depth of his fury.

"But why François? Why my diner?" she asked, her voice trembling.

Loki's laughter was cold and bitter. "François was renowned for his culinary prowess, his ability to create dishes that seemed almost...magical. He had to be stopped before he uncovered even more of our secrets. And your diner? It sits at a crossroads, a nexus of power. With François gone and you under my control, I can use this place as a gateway to spread my influence far and wide."

Spectres and Souffles

Sabrina's mind reeled as she struggled to process Loki's revelations. A centuries-old grudge against chefs? A plot to seize control of her diner? It was too much to take in. She shook her head, trying to clear the fog of confusion and fear.

"No," she said, her voice growing stronger. "I won't let you use my diner for your twisted schemes. I won't be a pawn in your game."

Loki's eyes flashed with amusement. "Oh, but you already are, my dear. You just don't realize it yet."

He leaned in close, his breath hot against her ear. "You have no idea what you've stumbled into, Sabrina Spellworth. But you will soon enough. And when you do, you'll beg for my mercy."

With that, he vanished in a swirl of smoke, leaving Sabrina alone in the kitchen, her heart pounding and her mind racing with questions she feared she might never answer. What had she gotten herself into? And more importantly, how was she going to stop a god?

Sabrina stood frozen, her eyes fixed on the spot where Eliot—no, Loki—had vanished. The air crackled with residual energy, a tangible reminder of the god's presence. She drew a shaky breath, the scent of dish soap and burnt sage mingling in her nostrils.

"Think, Sabrina, think," she muttered, running a hand through her hair. She couldn't let Loki win, couldn't let him use her diner as a conduit for his nefarious plans. But how could she stop a god?

She paced the kitchen, her mind racing. Loki had orchestrated François's death, manipulated events to suit his own agenda. The depth of his deceit and the lengths he'd gone to were staggering. And now, with the truth laid bare, she couldn't help but feel a twinge of guilt. If only she'd seen through his façade sooner...

"No," Sabrina said, her voice echoing in the empty kitchen. "I won't let him win. I won't let him corrupt this place, not after everything I've built here."

She thought of her customers, both living and dead, who had found solace and acceptance within the walls of the Crossroads Diner. She thought of the laughter, the tears, the shared moments that had made this place more than just a restaurant. It was a sanctuary, a beacon of hope in a world that often felt cold and unforgiving.

Sabrina squared her shoulders. She would find a way to stop Loki.

With a flick of her wrist, she summoned a spectral notepad and pen. "Time to call in some favors," she murmured, scribbling furiously. "If Loki wants a fight, he's got one."

She paused, tapping the pen against her chin. "But first, I need answers. And I know just where to start."

Sabrina strode out of the kitchen, the notepad clutched tightly in her hand. The Crossroads Diner hummed with energy, the air thick with the promise of secrets yet to be uncovered. She had a long road ahead of her, but one thing was certain: Sabrina Spellworth was not going down without a fight.

Eliot's towering figure cast an ominous shadow over Sabrina, his otherworldly aura pulsating with an intensity that sent shivers down her spine. The air crackled with a palpable tension, as if the very fabric of reality was straining under the weight of his presence. Sabrina's heart raced, her breath coming in short, sharp gasps as she fought to maintain her composure in the face of the ancient trickster god.

"Why, Eliot?" Sabrina's voice trembled, a mix of fear and determination lacing her words. "Why go to such lengths? What could possibly justify taking an innocent life?"

Eliot's eyes, now glowing with an ethereal light, fixed upon her with intensity. "Innocent?" He scoffed, his voice echoing with the weight of centuries. "The culinary world is far from innocent, Sabrina. It is a realm of deceit, of betrayal, of egos so inflated they threaten to block out the very sun."

Sabrina shook her head, refusing to accept his twisted logic. "And that gives you the right to play judge, jury, and executioner? To take matters into your own hands and destroy lives as you see fit?"

"You don't understand," Eliot hissed, his form shimmering with barely contained power. "The chefs, the critics, the so-called experts... they wield their influence like a weapon, crushing the dreams and aspirations of countless individuals. They revel in their own self-importance, blind to the destruction they leave in their wake."

Sabrina's mind whirled as she grappled with the weight of Eliot's bitterness. She recalled the countless spirits who had drifted through the Crossroads Diner, each carrying their own stories of dreams dashed and ambitions left to wither. Could Eliot's words hold a kernel of truth? Was there a shadow lurking beneath the glossy surface of the culinary world, a hidden rot festering beneath its glamorous facade?

"Even so," Sabrina pressed, her voice gaining strength with each word, "there are better ways to spark change than through bloodshed and ruin. You could have wielded your power to uncover the truth, to expose the injustices hiding in the shadows."

Eliot's laugh echoed through the room, cold and void of humor. "You think truth matters in a world where power is the only currency? Where influence is king? Truth is nothing but a nuisance, an inconvenient footnote to be buried."

Sabrina's fists clenched at her sides, her resolve hardening like tempered steel. "I won't let you continue this path of destruction, Eliot. I refuse to stand by while you tear apart the heart of this community."

Eliot's sneer deepened, his eyes glinting with mockery. "And what will you do, little ghost whisperer?" His tone dripped with condescension. "You may have sway over the dead, but I am a god. Your petty tricks are nothing against the might of a trickster.

Sabrina's eyes narrowed, a quiet, ancient power stirring beneath the surface. "You underestimate me, Eliot," she said, her voice low but unwavering. "You underestimate the power of those who've crossed beyond the veil—and the strength of a community united by purpose."

She stepped forward, her aura igniting with a radiant, otherworldly glow. The air around them crackled with energy, as if even the molecules sensed the shift in power. For a brief moment, Eliot's arrogant facade flickered, a glimmer of doubt flashing in his eyes.

"This ends now," Sabrina's voice rang out, steady and commanding. "You will answer for your crimes. The truth of François's death will be revealed, and the culinary world will know what you've done."

Eliot's expression darkened, his eyes gleaming with menace. His form shimmered, as if preparing to unleash all the power at his disposal. "We shall see, Sabrina Spellsworth," he growled, his voice thick with malice. "We shall see."

The air between them crackled with an unspoken tension as Eliot and Sabrina stood locked in a silent battle of wills. Eliot's eyes narrowed, his words steeped in arrogance. "You foolish little witch," he sneered. "Do you really think your paltry notions of justice can stop me? I am an ancient god, driven by a grudge that stretches back for centuries. Your mortal understanding of right and wrong is laughable compared to the depth of my vengeance."

Sabrina's heart pounded in her chest, fully aware of the danger Eliot represented. His power was vast, and she knew she was standing on precarious ground. Yet, a fierce determination surged within her—protecting the Crossroads Diner and the people whose lives depended on it was all that mattered.

"Your grudge is misplaced, Eliot," Sabrina said, her voice steadier now, though her body trembled under the weight of his presence. "The culinary world isn't your enemy. These chefs, these artists, pour their souls into their craft. They don't just cook—they create joy, comfort, connection. How can you justify destroying something that brings so much meaning to so many?"

Eliot's laughter reverberated through the room, cold and hollow. It sent a chill through Sabrina's spine. "Meaning?" he echoed, disdain dripping from his voice. "Essential? You mortals cling to such shallow concepts. The culinary world is nothing more than a cesspool of ego and vanity. These so-called chefs, with their bloated sense of importance, believe they are gods among men. Watching them fall... watching their world crumble to dust—nothing will bring me more satisfaction."

Sabrina's resolve tightened, and though Eliot's words chilled her, they also lit a fire. She wasn't just facing an ancient being bent on revenge—she was facing an idea as old as time itself: destruction for destruction's sake. And she refused to let it win.

A storm of emotions churned within Sabrina—fear, resolve, and something deeper she couldn't quite name. She knew retreat wasn't an option, that she couldn't allow Eliot's warped vision to triumph. But how could she, a mere mortal with a talent for speaking to the dead, possibly stand against the power of a trickster god?

As if sensing her inner turmoil, Eliot's lips curled into a smirk. "Poor little Sabrina, in over her head. You have no idea what you're up against. I have orchestrated the downfall of empires, toppled kings from their thrones. What chance do you think you have against me?"

Sabrina's hands clenched into fists, her fingernails digging into her palms. She drew in a deep breath, summoning every ounce of courage and resolve she possessed. "I may not have your power, Eliot, but I have something far greater. I have the strength of those who have passed on, the wisdom of generations, and the love of a community that will stand united against your malice."

She took a step forward, her eyes locked with Eliot's, a silent challenge hanging in the air between them. The fate of the Crossroads Diner, and perhaps even the culinary world itself, hung in the balance. Sabrina knew that the battle had only just begun, and she would need every ounce of her wit, courage, and otherworldly abilities to emerge victorious.

Eliot's laughter echoed through the room, a chilling sound that sent shivers down Sabrina's spine. The trickster god's eyes gleamed with malevolent amusement as he circled her, his footsteps eerily silent on the hardwood floor. "How touching, Sabrina. Your little speech about love and community. But do you really think that will be enough to stop me?"

Sabrina refused to let her fear show. She had faced countless challenges in her life, both from the living and the dead, and she had always found a way to overcome them. This time would be no different. She drew herself up to her full height, her vintage dress swishing around her legs as she faced Eliot head-on.

"I know it will be enough, Eliot. Because I'm not alone. I have the support of every soul who has ever passed through the doors of the Crossroads Diner. They believe in me, just as I believe in them. And together, we will put an end to your twisted vendetta."

Eliot's eyes narrowed, his aura pulsing with barely contained rage. "You dare to defy me, mortal? You, who are nothing more than a meddlesome woman with a gift for talking to ghosts? I will crush you like an insect beneath my heel."

Eliot's eyes widened, his arrogant smirk faltering as Sabrina's words hit their mark. He took a step back, his towering form seeming to diminish slightly in the face of her unwavering resolve. "You... you're not afraid of me?" he asked, confusion and surprise lacing his ethereal voice.

Sabrina shook her head, a small, triumphant smile tugging at the corners of her lips. "No, Eliot. I'm not afraid of you. I'm afraid for you. Afraid of what will happen if you continue down this path of hatred and revenge."

She took another step forward. "I know you've been hurt, Eliot. I know that the culinary world has wronged you in ways I can't even imagine. But this? This isn't the answer. Hurting others, taking innocent lives... it won't heal your pain. It'll only make it worse."

Eliot's eyes narrowed, his jaw clenching as he struggled to maintain his composure. "You know nothing of my pain, mortal," he hissed, his voice dripping with venom. "You cannot possibly understand the depths of my rage, the centuries of injustice I have endured."

But even as he spoke, Sabrina could see the cracks forming in his armor, the flickers of doubt and uncertainty that danced behind his glowing eyes. She pressed on, her voice growing stronger with each word. "You're right, Eliot. I don't understand your pain. But I do understand the power of forgiveness, of letting go of the past and embracing a better future."

She reached out her hand, palm up, a gesture of peace and understanding. "It's not too late, Eliot. You can still choose a different path. You can still find redemption, if you're willing to seek it."

For a long moment, Eliot stared at her outstretched hand, his expression unreadable. The air between them crackled with tension, the fate of the Crossroads Diner hanging in the balance. Then, slowly, almost imperceptibly, his fingers twitched, as if yearning to reach out and take her offer.

But before he could move, a sudden gust of wind tore through the diner, shattering the windows and sending shards of glass flying through the air. Sabrina threw up her hands to shield her face, her heart pounding in her chest as she heard Eliot's enraged roar echo through the chaos.

"Enough!" he bellowed, his voice shaking the very foundations of the building. "I will not be swayed by your pretty words and empty promises. I will have my revenge, and nothing, not even you, can stop me."

With a final, guttural snarl, Eliot lunged, his form distorting with a terrifying fluidity as he prepared to strike. Sabrina stood firm, though her mind raced to summon every last shred of her paranormal power. She could feel the weight of the moment pressing down on her, the fate of her beloved diner hanging in the balance.

A fierce wind whipped through the room, scattering napkins and menus like frantic birds. The scent of ozone and ancient magic filled the diner, a sharp contrast to the familiar, comforting aroma of apple pie that usually lingered in the air.

"Eliot, stop!" Sabrina's voice was barely audible above the howling gusts. "It doesn't have to be like this. We can find another way—together."

Eliot's eyes gleamed with a malevolent, unearthly light. His sneer deepened, venom dripping from his words. "You pathetic fool," he spat. "Do you think kindness can rewrite the laws of the universe? I have seen the truth, lived through centuries of betrayal and cruelty. The world is cold. Unforgiving. And so am I."

Sabrina's chest tightened at the bitterness that laced his voice. Beneath his rage, she glimpsed something more—a soul weathered by endless suffering. She could see it in the way he spoke, in the anger that masked his wounds. She knew, in that moment, she had to reach him. Somehow.

"It doesn't have to be that way," she whispered, taking a cautious step forward. The crunch of shattered glass underfoot reminded her of the destruction that had already unfolded. "We all have a choice, Eliot. Even you. To rise above the past, to create something better."

For the briefest moment, Eliot's form flickered, his presence wavering as though he was caught between worlds. And in that heartbeat, Sabrina saw something else—a glimmer of hesitation, a crack in his facade. The man he once was still lived beneath the layers of resentment.

But the moment passed in an instant, and with a roar of fury, Eliot surged forward, his hands crackling with dark energy. Sabrina barely managed to conjure a shield of shimmering light, deflecting the arcane blast. The force sent her skidding backward, her vintage dress tearing as she slammed into the counter.

"Sabrina!" Pepper's voice sliced through the storm of chaos as she burst through the kitchen doors, tattoos aglow with protective magic. François and Mort followed close behind, their ethereal forms brimming with intent.

As her friends gathered around her, Sabrina felt a wave of strength surge through her, something deeper than mere resolve. This wasn't just a battle for the Crossroads Diner. This was a battle for the soul of their world, for everything the paranormal community had built and cherished.

With a steadying breath, Sabrina pushed herself to her feet, locking eyes with Eliot's towering, crackling form. "This ends now," she declared, her voice carrying a force she had never known. "One way or another, we finish this."

The air thickened with tension as both sides braced for the final collision. The fate of the diner, and everyone within it, hung precariously on the edge of whatever came next. Whether Sabrina's love and light could reach the depths of Eliot's darkness was uncertain, but the battle had begun. And there was no turning back.

Chapter 14

Sabrina froze in her tracks as she entered the spectral kitchen, her eyes widening in disbelief at the twisted and distorted features that surrounded her. The once familiar appliances and countertops now appeared warped and menacing, their surfaces pulsing with an eerie, otherworldly glow. A chilling breeze swept through the room, carrying with it the faint whispers of tormented souls.

"Well, this is a fine mess we've gotten ourselves into," Mort quipped, his skeletal grin belying the unease in his hollow eye sockets. "I don't suppose anyone brought a recipe for 'Escape from Haunted Kitchen' casserole?"

Pepper's hands crackled with magical energy as she surveyed the nightmarish scene. "I'm pretty sure that dish requires ingredients we don't have on hand, like 'Courage' and 'A Way Out.'"

Sabrina shook her head, trying to clear the growing sense of dread that threatened to overwhelm her. She glanced at her companions and noticed the fear etched on their faces - even Boo, their ever-loyal spectral canine, seemed to shrink in the presence of the malevolent energy that permeated the kitchen.

Suddenly, the ground beneath them began to tremble, and the twisted appliances sprang to life, their doors and drawers slamming open and closed with a deafening cacophony. Knives, forks, and other utensils flew through the air, their sharp edges glinting menacingly in the eerie light.

"LOOK OUT!" Sabrina shouted as she dove to the side, narrowly avoiding a barrage of spectral spatulas that embedded themselves in the wall behind her.

As the chaos intensified, each team member found themselves face-to-face with manifestations of their deepest fears and insecurities.

The once-cozy kitchen had transformed into a hellish landscape, where the very essence of their beings was put to the test.

Mort ducked under a volley of ghostly rolling pins, his bones rattling with a mix of fear and determination. Pepper's hands glowed brighter as she conjured a shimmering shield to deflect the onslaught of possessed kitchenware. And poor Boo, the timid ghost dog, cowered behind Sabrina, his spectral form flickering in and out of existence.

"We need to stick together!" Sabrina called out, her voice barely audible over the deafening clamor. She reached for her friends, desperate to maintain some semblance of unity in the face of this unimaginable horror.

As the team huddled close, their eyes darting frantically around the nightmarish kitchen, a chilling realization dawned upon them: this was only the beginning of the trials that lay ahead. With each passing moment, the spectral kitchen seemed to grow more sinister, its twisted features pulsing with malevolent energy.

How long could they withstand the onslaught of their own fears and insecurities made manifest? And more importantly, would they be able to uncover the dark secrets that lurked within the heart of this ghostly realm before it consumed them entirely?

The clock ticked relentlessly as darkness closed in, trapping them in a chilling race against the malevolent forces consuming the kitchen and a twisted mastermind's vengeful plots.

Sabrina's heart raced as she found herself separated from the group, the spectral kitchen's twisting corridors seemingly closing in around her. The once familiar pots and pans now took on a sinister appearance, their surfaces warped and distorted like funhouse mirrors.

"Come on, Sabrina," she muttered to herself, her voice trembling slightly. "You've communicated with hundreds of spirits before. This is just another challenge to overcome."

As if in response to her words, a ghostly whisper filled the air, its icy tendrils snaking into her mind. "But what if you fail?" the voice taunted. "What if you lead your friends astray and condemn them to an eternity in this nightmarish realm?"

Sabrina's breath caught in her throat as a luminous figure materialized before her—a twisted reflection of herself, its eyes gleaming with malice. The doppelganger's vintage dress was tattered and stained, its once vibrant colors now muted and gray.

"You're not real," Sabrina declared, her hands balling into fists at her sides. "You're just a manifestation of my fears."

The spectral double laughed, a harsh, grating sound that sent shivers down Sabrina's spine. "Oh, but I am real," it crooned. "I'm the part of you that knows the truth—that you're not strong enough to save your friends or solve this mystery."

Sabrina's mind raced as she tried to find the right words to banish the apparition, but doubt crept in, its icy fingers gripping her heart.

Meanwhile, Mort found himself in a cavernous chamber, its walls lined with mirrors that reflected his skeletal form back at him in endless iterations. The air hung heavy with the weight of centuries, and the scent of decay permeated the space.

"Huh," he mused, his voice echoing in the eerie stillness. "I've spent eons guiding others to the afterlife, but I've never really considered my own mortality."

As he stepped closer to one of the mirrors, a figure emerged from the depths of the glass—a spectral reaper, its form identical to his own, save for the pulsing, sickly green light that emanated from its eye sockets.

"You may guide others to their eternal rest," the figure intoned, its voice a hollow whisper, "but what awaits you when your own time comes?"

Mort's grip tightened on his scythe as he stared into the reaper's glowing eyes. "I've always assumed I'd just fade away," he replied, his usual sarcasm tinged with uncertainty. "No grand finale, no encore. Just a one-way ticket to oblivion."

The spectral reaper tilted its head, a mocking gesture that sent a chill through Mort's bones. "But what if there's something more?" it whispered. "Something beyond the veil that even you, the great and powerful Reaper, cannot comprehend?"

As Mort grappled with the unsettling prospect of his own uncertain fate, a sudden, anguished scream echoed through the chamber. The sound was unmistakable—Sabrina was in trouble!

Without a second thought, Mort turned to rush to his friend's aid, but as he did, the floor beneath him shifted and warped, forcing him to stop cold. Another scream pierced the air as he struggled to maintain his balance. Could he reach Sabrina in time or would his own crisis trap him while she faced unknown perils alone?

Pepper's hands crackled with arcane energy as she faced the onslaught of animated kitchenware. Whisks whirled like miniature tornadoes, spatulas sliced through the air like blades, and a battalion of possessed rolling pins advanced menacingly, their wooden bodies creaking with each rotation.

"Alright, you culinary creeps," Pepper declared, her eyes narrowing with determination. "Time to whip you into shape!"

She thrust her hands forward, channeling her magic into a concentrated blast. The spell surged towards the approaching kitchenware, but at the last moment, it veered off course, ricocheting off a nearby pot and narrowly missing Boo, who yelped in surprise.

"Oops! Sorry, Boo!" Pepper called out, wincing at her misfired spell. "I'm still working on my aim."

The ghostly dog gave a forgiving bark before turning his attention back to the spectral creatures that had begun to materialize around him. Translucent, distorted shapes took form, their features twisted and grotesque. Boo's ears flattened against his head as he backed away, a whimper escaping his throat.

"I... I don't know if I can do this," he thought, his spectral tail tucking between his legs. "I'm just a little ghost dog. How can I protect anyone?"

As if sensing his fear, one of the creatures lunged forward, its jaws snapping mere inches from Boo's face. The ghost dog let out a startled bark, instinctively leaping back. His ethereal fur stood on end.

With a bark, Boo charged forward, his spectral form phasing through the creature's body. The twisted being let out a shriek of surprise as Boo's essence disrupted its own, causing it to flicker and dissipate momentarily.

Meanwhile, Pepper found herself surrounded by a whirlwind of possessed kitchenware, her spells flying erratically in every direction. Pots and pans clattered to the floor, and a bag of flour burst open, creating a hazy cloud that filled the air.

"Ack! I can't see a thing!" Pepper coughed, waving her hand in front of her face to clear the flour from her vision. "Where's a good wind spell when you need one?"

Spectres and Souffles

As she stumbled through the chaos, Pepper's foot caught on a stray rolling pin, sending her tumbling to the ground. She landed hard, the breath knocked from her lungs. The animated kitchenware closed in, their shadows looming over her prone form.

Pepper's mind raced, searching for a solution. Her spells were too unpredictable, too dangerous in such close quarters. She needed a new approach, something that could turn the tide of this culinary catastrophe.

Her gaze fell upon a nearby oven, its door slightly ajar. A flicker of an idea sparked in her mind, and a mischievous grin spread across her face. If she could just lure the possessed objects inside...

With a determined grunt, Pepper pushed herself to her feet, her hands aglow with arcane energy. She had a plan, but she knew she'd only have one shot to make it work. The fate of her friends—and perhaps the entire spectral kitchen—hung in the balance.

Sabrina ducked as a possessed whisk whizzed past her head, narrowly missing her by a hair's breadth. "Pepper!" she called out, her voice strained with concern. "Are you alright?"

"I'm fine!" Pepper shouted back, dodging a barrage of animated cutlery. "But we need to regroup! I have an idea!"

Mort, who had been grappling with a particularly aggressive rolling pin, managed to wrestle the object into submission. "I'm all ears, Red," he quipped, his skeletal grin somehow conveying both amusement and exasperation.

Boo, meanwhile, found himself cornered by a menacing group of spectral spatulas. The ghost dog's fur stood on end as he let out a series of frantic barks, his eyes wide with fear.

Sabrina's heart ached at the sight of her faithful companion in distress. She knew she had to act fast. With a burst of adrenalen, she closed her eyes and focused her energy on the bond she shared with Boo. "It's okay, boy," she whispered, her voice filled with warmth and reassurance. "We're in this together."

As if sensing his mistress's encouragement, Boo's posture straightened, and a newfound courage flickered in his ghostly eyes. With a bark, he charged forward, phasing through the spectral spatulas and causing them to dissipate in a wisp of ectoplasmic smoke.

Pepper, seeing an opening, beckoned her friends toward the oven. "Quick, over here!" she urged, her voice thick with urgency. "If we can lure these kitchen creeps inside, I think I can contain them!"

Mort and Sabrina exchanged a quick glance—skeptical, but not hesitant. They knew better than to question Pepper's methods; she had a knack for the unconventional. Trust in her abilities, however odd, outweighed their doubts. With a shared nod, they braced themselves and set to work, corralling the possessed kitchenware toward the oven. It was a chaotic, absurd task, but they had no choice but to meet it head-on.

Sabrina approached with a steady calm, channeling her empathy into the tangled emotions clinging to the animated objects. She spoke in soothing tones, coaxing them with a gentle understanding only she could offer. Mort, by contrast, took an entirely different approach—his towering figure and biting wit were enough to cow even the most rebellious of utensils. His dry humor cut through the frenzy, intimidating the objects into submission with an air of sarcastic authority.

The two worked in seamless unison, their bond tightening with each passing moment. Trust wasn't just implied—it was instinctive. Mort and Sabrina moved as one, predicting each other's actions with unspoken precision. Their connection, forged in the midst of chaos, felt like second nature as they deftly adapted to the erratic environment of the spectral kitchen.

But as they made headway, the battle grew fiercer. The possessed objects turned vicious, their erratic movements becoming wild, hostile. Knives swirled in the air like deadly darts, pans thudded against counters with malicious intent. Sabrina could feel the toll—the strain of controlling so many agitated entities pulled at her, her energy depleting rapidly. Her usually calm exterior began to falter as exhaustion crept in, her emphatic reach stretched thin.

Mort, too, was unraveling. His usual stoic confidence gave way to frustration, the weight of their escalating predicament visible in the tension of his ghostly form. For the first time, his dry humor wavered as he struggled to keep pace with the relentless assault of objects that refused to bend to his will.

Spectres and Souffles

Pepper, too, felt the strain of their ordeal. Her magical reserves dwindled, and her confidence wavered in the face of the relentless onslaught. But she refused to give up, drawing strength from the unwavering support of her friends.

As the last of the possessed objects clattered into the oven, Pepper slammed the door shut, her hands aglow with the remnants of her magical energy. The oven shuddered and shook, the temperature gauge spinning wildly as the witch poured every ounce of her power into the containment spell.

For a moment, the spectral kitchen fell silent, the air heavy with anticipation. Sabrina, Mort, and Boo watched in breathless suspense, their faith in Pepper's abilities unwavering.

And then, with a final, resounding click, the oven door sealed itself shut, the ghostly glow of the possessed objects fading behind the reinforced glass. Pepper staggered back, her face pale and her breathing ragged, but a triumphant smile tugged at the corners of her lips.

"It worked," she gasped, her voice barely above a whisper. "We did it."

But as the team gathered around their exhausted friend, a creeping sense of unease began to settle over them. The spectral kitchen, though momentarily subdued, seemed to pulse with a malevolent energy, as if Eliot's power still lingered in the shadows.

They had won the battle, but the war was far from over. And as they stood together, their bond stronger than ever, they knew that the true test of their resilience and determination was yet to come.

Sabrina's eyes darted around the spectral kitchen, her intuition telling her that something wasn't quite right. The eerie calm that had settled over the room felt like the eye of a hurricane, a brief respite before the storm unleashed its fury once more.

"We need to keep moving," she said, her voice steady despite the growing sense of unease. "Eliot's not going to give up that easily."

Mort nodded, his skeletal fingers tightening around the handle of his scythe. "Agreed. We've bought ourselves some time, but we need to use it wisely."

As if on cue, a faint whisper echoed through the kitchen, the sound sending a chill down Sabrina's spine. It was a voice she recognized all too well—Eliot's voice, taunting them from the shadows.

"You think you've won, don't you?" the voice hissed, the words dripping with malice. "But you're merely pawns in a game far beyond your comprehension."

Pepper's eyes narrowed, her tattoos glowing with renewed energy. "We're not afraid of you, Eliot," she declared, her voice ringing with defiance. "We'll find a way to stop you, no matter what it takes."

Boo let out a low, determined bark, his ghostly tail wagging in agreement. Sabrina couldn't help but smile at the sight, her heart swelling with pride at the bravery of her friends.

But as they moved deeper into the spectral kitchen, the challenges that awaited them grew more daunting by the moment. The twisted corridors seemed to shift and change, leading them down a labyrinth of nightmarish visions and distorted realities.

Sabrina's mind raced, searching for a solution, a clue, anything that might help them escape this hellish landscape. And then, out of the corner of her eye, she spotted something—a flicker of movement, a shadow that seemed to beckon them forward.

"There," she whispered, pointing towards the anomaly. "Do you see that?"

Mort's eye sockets narrowed, his gaze following Sabrina's outstretched finger. "I do," he murmured, his voice tinged with curiosity. "It almost looks like..."

"A way out," Pepper finished, her eyes wide with realization. "But how?"

Sabrina shook her head, her brow furrowed in concentration. "I don't know," she admitted, "but it's the best lead we've got. We have to follow it."

And then, just as they were about to step into the unknown, a deafening roar shook the very foundations of the kitchen, the sound reverberating through their bones like a seismic wave. The team whirled around, their eyes wide with horror as they beheld the sight before them.

There, emerging from the depths of the spectral kitchen, was a monstrous figure, its form twisted and distorted by the malevolent energy that pulsed through the room. Its eyes blazed with an unearthly fire, its maw filled with razor-sharp teeth that gleamed in the eerie light.

Sabrina desperately searched for a way to overcome the monstrous figure that loomed before them. She glanced at her companions, their faces etched with a mixture of fear and determination, and in that moment, a surge of strength coursed through her veins.

"We can't let this thing stop us,"

Mort nodded."Sabrina's right. We've faced our fears and grown stronger because of it. This is just another obstacle we have to overcome."

Pepper's hands crackled with magical energy, her eyes narrowing as she assessed the creature. "I may not have full control over my powers, but I'll be damned if I let this monstrosity hurt any of you."

Boo let out a bark, his spectral tail wagging with a fierce resolve. He positioned himself in front of the team.

As they stood united, the very air around them seemed to shift, the oppressive atmosphere lightening ever so slightly. The monstrous figure let out another ear-splitting roar, its claws scraping against the fractured tiles of the kitchen floor.

Sabrina's eyes darted around the room, searching for anything that could give them an advantage. And then, in the midst of the chaos, she spotted it—a faint glimmer of light emanating from a crack in the wall behind the creature.

"There!" she shouted, pointing towards the anomaly. "That might be our way out!"

The team exchanged glances, a silent understanding passing between them. They knew that reaching the potential escape route would be no easy feat, but they were ready to face whatever challenges lay ahead.

With a rallying cry, they charged forward, their unique abilities and unwavering determination propelling them towards the monstrous figure. The creature lunged at them, its claws slashing through the air with deadly precision, but the team moved as one, dodging and weaving with a newfound grace.

Sabrina's spirit-sensing abilities allowed her to anticipate the creature's movements, guiding her friends to safety as they pressed on.

Mort's ghostly form phased through the monster's attacks, creating openings for Pepper to unleash bursts of magical energy that sent the creature reeling.

And Boo, the once-timid ghost dog, leaped into action, his spectral jaws clamping down on the monster's leg, distracting it long enough for the team to gain ground.

As they neared the glimmering light, the creature let out a final, desperate roar, its form beginning to dissolve under the onslaught of the team's combined efforts. Sabrina reached out, her fingers brushing against the crack in the wall, and suddenly, the world around them began to shift and blur.

The spectral kitchen faded away, replaced by a swirling vortex of energy that pulled at them with an irresistible force. The team clung to one another, their hearts pounding as they were drawn into the unknown, the monstrous figure's echoing roar fading into the distance.

And then, just as suddenly as it had begun, the vortex dissipated, and the team found themselves standing in a place that defied description—a realm where the past, present, and future collided in a kaleidoscope of possibility.

As they caught their breath, Sabrina looked around, her eyes widening with a mixture of awe and trepidation. "Where are we?" she whispered, her voice echoing in the strange, timeless space.

But before anyone could answer, a figure emerged from the shadows, its form flickering and shifting like a mirage. And as it drew closer, Sabrina's heart skipped a beat, for standing before them was none other than Eliot Drayton himself, his eyes filled with an unsettling intensity.

"Welcome," he said, his voice low and measured, "to the place where all secrets are revealed, and all destinies are decided."

Chapter 15

The amber glow of the setting sun filtered through the lace curtains of Sabrina's office, casting elongated shadows across her desk. She sat hunched in her chair, elbows propped on the worn wooden surface, face buried in her hands. The weight of her failed attempt to reach François pressed down on her shoulders like a lead blanket.

"Why did I think he would listen?" she muttered to herself, a mirthless chuckle escaping her lips. "Silly me, believing in the power of nostalgia and friendship."

Sabrina's fingers fumbled with the top drawer of her desk, her hands trembling as she retrieved a faded photograph. In the picture, a younger Sabrina and François stood arm-in-arm, their faces alight with laughter and the promise of a bright future together. How times had changed.

She clutched the photo to her chest, a bittersweet reminder of the hope she once harbored for their partnership. François had been her rock, her confidant, and her partner in both life and business. Together, they had transformed the Crossroads Diner from a struggling greasy spoon into a thriving paranormal hotspot.

But now, as Sabrina stared at the smiling faces in the photograph, doubt crept into her mind like an uninvited guest. Had she been foolish to trust him so completely? Was her gift, her ability to communicate with the departed, nothing more than a parlor trick in his eyes?

The creaking of the office door jolted Sabrina from her ruminations...

The sound of footsteps approaching the office door interrupted Sabrina's thoughts. She quickly wiped away her tears with the back of her hand, the photograph falling onto the desk. Straightening her shoulders,

Sabrina took a deep breath and plastered a brave smile on her face, determined to maintain a strong front for her team.

The door swung open, revealing Mort's towering figure in the doorway. His black robes billowed around him as he stepped into the office, his scythe gleaming in the dim light. Concern etched on his skeletal face, Mort's glowing eye sockets fixed on Sabrina, taking in her distress.

"Sabrina, my dear," Mort spoke, his ethereal voice tinged with worry. "I couldn't help but notice the storm clouds gathering over your head. What's troubling you?"

Sabrina's smile faltered, her eyes glistening with unshed tears. "Oh, Mort," she sighed, her shoulders sagging. "It's just... I thought I could reach François, make him see reason. But I failed."

Mort glided across the room, his robes whispering against the hardwood floor. He gently placed a bony hand on Sabrina's shoulder, offering her a comforting smile. The gesture, though cold to the touch, radiated a warmth that seeped into Sabrina's heart.

"Now, now," Mort chuckled, his eyes sparkling with mischief. "Since when has failure ever stopped the indomitable Sabrina Spellsworth? You've faced far worse than a stubborn ex-partner with a superiority complex."

Sabrina couldn't help but laugh, the sound chasing away some of the gloom that had settled over her. "You're right, Mort. I can't let this setback define me."

Mort nodded sagely, his scythe bobbing in agreement. "Precisely! And besides, you've got a team of loyal misfits ready to stand by your side. We'll figure this out, just like we always do."

Sabrina's smile grew more genuine as she looked up at Mort with gratitude.

Sabrina took a deep breath, the weight on her shoulders feeling a little lighter. She straightened her vintage dress and squared her shoulders, ready to face the challenges ahead.

"I just can't help but feel like my abilities have let me down," she confessed, her voice still tinged with doubt. "What if I'm not strong enough to protect the diner and everyone who depends on it?"

Mort's expression softened, his sardonic demeanor replaced by genuine empathy. He leaned forward, his voice low and earnest. "Sabrina, your gift is a part of who you are. It's what makes you special, what allows you to create this haven for lost souls."

He gestured around the office, the walls adorned with photographs of smiling patrons, both living and dead. "Look at all the lives you've touched, the difference you've made. That's not something to doubt, it's something to celebrate."

Sabrina's eyes followed Mort's gesture, taking in the memories captured in each frame. She felt a warmth blossoming in her chest, a renewed sense of purpose.

"You're right, Mort," she said, her voice growing stronger with each word. "I can't let one setback make me question everything I've built here."

Mort's skeletal grin widened, his eye sockets glowing with pride. "That's the spirit! Now, let's put our heads together and come up with a plan to save this little slice of paranormal paradise."

A flicker of inspiration danced in Mort's eye sockets as he leaned forward, his bony elbows resting on Sabrina's desk. "You know, we might be overlooking a valuable resource here," he mused, his voice tinged with excitement.

Sabrina tilted her head, curiosity piqued. "What do you mean?"

"The spirits," Mort said, his grin widening. "The ones who frequent this fine establishment. They've seen things, heard things... who knows what kind of juicy gossip they might have on François?"

Sabrina's eyes widened, a glimmer of hope igniting within them. "You think they could help us?"

"It's worth a shot," Mort shrugged, his robes rustling with the movement. "And who better to connect with them than the one and only Sabrina Spellsworth, medium extraordinaire?"

A smile tugged at the corners of Sabrina's lips, her earlier doubts beginning to dissipate. "A séance," she breathed, the idea taking root in her mind. "We could hold a séance right here in the diner, invite the spirits to share what they know."

Mort nodded, his skull bobbing with enthusiasm. "Exactly! And with your gift, you'll be able to communicate with them like no one else can."

Sabrina rose abruptly, the hem of her vintage dress brushing against her knees as she paced the cramped office, her mind racing through possibilities. Suddenly, she stopped mid-stride and turned to face Mort, resolve sharpening her gaze.

"We're doing it," she declared, her voice clear and firm. "I've been so wrapped up in my own abilities that I forgot we have an invaluable resource right here—the souls that make this place what it is."

Mort stood, his scythe flickering into his grip as if summoned by thought alone. "That's the spirit, Sabrina! Pun fully intended."

She chuckled, the tension in the room lifting with her laughter. Mort was right. She needed to stop doubting herself and lean into the support of her team—both living and dead.

Together, they moved out of the office, the familiar sights of the diner grounding her as they gathered their team. Sabrina felt a new sense of purpose thrumming beneath her skin. The spirits had always been there for her, but now, she would be calling on them in a way she never had before.

Little did she realize, tonight's séance would unlock far more than just clues about François—it would ignite a series of events that would push her beyond the limits of what she thought possible.

As dusk bled into twilight, painting the sky in soft strokes of pink and orange, Sabrina and Mort convened with Pepper and Boo in the diner's main dining area. The usual low hum of ghostly conversations had fallen silent, replaced by an undercurrent of anticipation. The air felt thick, almost electric, brimming with secrets eager to be uncovered.

"Alright, team," Sabrina began, her eyes flashing with determination. "We're conducting a séance tonight. It's time to seek guidance from the spirits—they've always been our allies, and now we need them more than ever."

Pepper's eyes lit up like she'd just been given the best news of her life. "A séance? Hell yes! I've been itching to test out some of my new spells."

Boo let out a soft, eager bark, his spectral tail wagging. Sabrina smiled at the little ghost dog's enthusiasm—he always seemed ready for adventure.

Spectres and Souffles

As they cleared the center of the diner, setting up candles and preparing for the ritual, Sabrina's thoughts flickered with hope and doubt in equal measure. Could the spirits really hold the answers she needed to stop François? Was there a key to saving the diner hidden within the ghostly whispers of the beyond?

Sensing her uncertainty, Mort placed a hand on her shoulder, his voice calm and steady. "Remember, you don't face this alone. We've got your back—both the living and the dead."

Sabrina nodded, drawing in a deep breath to focus herself. The séance would demand everything from her, but with her team standing alongside her, she felt ready—at least as ready as one could be for the unknown.

The last rays of sunlight faded completely, plunging the diner into a hushed twilight. Candles flickered, their shadows dancing across the walls, casting an eerie glow over the room. The team took their places around the table, the quiet weight of expectation settling over them. Boo curled up at Sabrina's feet, his spectral presence offering a sense of comfort as they prepared for whatever revelations the spirits might unveil.

Pepper, her red hair glowing like a halo in the candlelight, grinned at Sabrina. "Let's do this, boss. Time to show those spirits who's boss."

Sabrina chuckled, feeling the tension in her shoulders ease. "Alright, everyone, let's begin."

The team joined hands, their eyes closing as Sabrina began to speak, her voice low and steady. The air in the diner seemed to still, the only sound the soft crackling of the candles.

As Sabrina's words filled the room, calling out to the spirits, a chill ran down her spine. She could feel the energy shifting, the veil between the living and the dead growing thinner with each passing moment.

Just as she was about to continue, a sudden gust of wind swept through the diner, extinguishing the candles and plunging the room into darkness. Boo let out a startled bark, and Pepper gasped, her grip tightening on Sabrina's hand.

In the shadows, Sabrina's heart pounded, her mind swirling with thoughts of what the spirits might unveil. Unbeknownst to her, the séance was on the verge of a revelation none of them could have anticipated—

one that would challenge not only their abilities but the strength of their bond as a team.

The darkness seemed to stretch on for an eternity, broken only by the sound of Sabrina's voice, now tinged with uncertainty. "Is anyone there? We've come seeking guidance and wisdom."

Seconds ticked by, each one feeling like an hour. Sabrina's palms grew clammy, and she could feel Mort's hand trembling slightly in her own. The silence was deafening, and doubt began to creep into her mind. What if the spirits didn't answer? What if she'd led her team on a wild goose chase?

Suddenly, a faint whisper echoed through the room, barely audible at first. Sabrina strained her ears, trying to make out the words. The whisper grew louder, and she realized it was coming from all around them, as if the spirits were speaking in unison.

"Sabrina," the voices whispered, their tone urgent. "You must not lose hope. The answer lies within the heart of the Crossroads Diner."

Sabrina's brow furrowed, her mind racing to make sense of the cryptic message. "What do you mean? Please, we need your help to save the diner."

The whispers intensified, their words overlapping and blending together until Sabrina could barely distinguish one from another. She caught snippets of phrases, each one more puzzling than the last.

"The key to your success lies in the past."

"Trust in the bonds you've forged."

"The truth will be revealed when the time is right."

As quickly as they had begun, the whispers faded away, leaving Sabrina and her team once again in silence. The candles flickered back to life, casting an eerie glow over their faces.

Sabrina let out a shaky breath, her mind reeling with the implications of the spirits' words. She turned to her team, her eyes wide with a mix of excitement and trepidation.

"Did you hear that?" she asked, her voice barely above a whisper.

Mort nodded, his expression thoughtful. "It seems the spirits are on our side, but their message was rather cryptic."

Pepper leaned forward, her eyes sparkling with curiosity. "What do you think they meant by 'the answer lies within the heart of the Crossroads Diner'?"

Sabrina shook her head, a small smile playing on her lips. "I'm not sure, but I have a feeling we're about to embark on a journey of discovery. The spirits have given us a clue, and it's up to us to unravel the mystery."

The séance was supposed to be the turning point. Sabrina hadn't expected things to spiral so quickly from cryptic whispers to outright chaos, but here they were, standing on the precipice of something far larger than any of them could have anticipated. As she paced the office, the weight of the spirits' message settled heavily on her shoulders, but it also fueled a fire within her—a need to uncover the diner's long-buried secrets, no matter the cost.

Sabrina stopped mid-step, turning toward Mort, her eyes alight with purpose. "Alright, we have work to do. The spirits gave us a starting point, but it's up to us to figure out what they meant. We're not just waiting around for answers. We dig."

Mort smirked, resting his hands on the scythe that had appeared at his side. "Well, we could always turn the place inside out—maybe there's a secret treasure map under a floorboard," he quipped, though his usual sarcastic bite was tinged with focus.

"Or," Pepper interjected, her brows knit together in thought, "what if the 'heart of the Crossroads Diner' isn't something physical? What if it's metaphorical—something tied to the diner's essence, its history?"

Sabrina nodded slowly, turning Pepper's words over in her mind. "That's possible. The diner's always been a bridge between the living and the dead, a place where stories and memories linger. Maybe the answer is buried in the connections that have been made here over the years."

Boo, who had been watching silently from the side, suddenly perked up, his ghostly tail flicking. "What about the jukebox?" he suggested, his small voice surprising them all. "It's been here since the diner opened—seen a lot of heartfelt moments, and plenty of ghostly ones, too."

Sabrina's eyes lit up. "Boo, that's brilliant! The jukebox has always been more than just a machine—it's woven into the very fabric of this place."

The group exchanged glances, excitement palpable as the prospect of a new lead energized them. They made their way toward the jukebox, Sabrina feeling a sense of anticipation curling through her veins. The diner's secrets were starting to unravel, and she was ready to meet whatever revelations lay ahead.

But as Sabrina neared the jukebox, something strange caught her eye. A faint glow emanated from the buttons, as if calling her forward. Her fingers trembled slightly as they hovered over the worn plastic, poised to uncover whatever the spirits had left behind.

Before she could make contact, a deafening crash from the kitchen shattered the stillness, sending everyone into a tense alert. The team whipped around, eyes wide with confusion and apprehension.

"What in the—?" Mort started, his scythe snapping to his side as he turned toward the sound.

Sabrina's pulse quickened. The mystery of the jukebox would have to wait. She glanced at the others, seeing the same mix of curiosity and fear reflected in their eyes. "Let's go," she said, her voice steadier than she felt. "Stay close."

They moved cautiously through the diner, pushing open the kitchen doors with trepidation. What greeted them on the other side left them speechless. The kitchen was a wreck—pots and pans littered the floor, while an oozing black substance dripped from the walls. The smell of sulfur and decay hung thick in the air, stinging their noses and making the room feel oppressive.

In the center of it all, a shape—no, a presence—shifted and writhed, its form a mass of undulating shadow.

"What the hell is that?" Pepper whispered, her voice barely a breath.

Sabrina's eyes narrowed as she took in the bizarre sight. "Whatever it is," she muttered, "it's not here to play nice."

The shadow twisted, its eyeless face turning toward them with an unsettling focus. It let out a deep, guttural growl, a sound that vibrated through their bones and sent icy shivers down their spines.

Mort stepped forward, his usual wit tempered by a cold edge. "Alright, you overgrown ink blot, you've got five seconds to explain yourself before I send you packing."

The shadow's form shimmered, and a voice—deep, unsettling—rippled through the room. "Fools. You meddle in forces beyond your reckoning. The secrets of the Crossroads Diner are not for the likes of you."

Spectres and Souffles

Sabrina refused to flinch. She'd faced down spirits, poltergeists, and worse. This thing—whatever it was—wouldn't push her around. "This is my diner," she said, her voice sharp with authority. "You don't get to make threats here."

The creature's body expanded, its inky tendrils reaching out toward them, filling the space with a growing darkness. The team instinctively closed ranks, their fear tightening the air around them as they realized the scale of what they were up against.

Sabrina's mind raced, searching for a way to fight back. Her eyes darted to a shelf in the corner—jars of herbs and spices sat lined up neatly, a flicker of an idea sparking in her brain. Without hesitation, she lunged toward the shelf, her fingers wrapping around jars of salt and sage.

Mort's voice cut through the tension. "Sabrina, whatever you're planning, now would be a great time to do it."

"I'm on it," she shot back, her heart pounding as she prepared to unleash whatever power she could muster.

"Everybody, get behind me!" Sabrina shouted, her voice cutting through the chaos. She thrust her hand forward, the mixture of salt and sage flying through the air and colliding with the shadow creature's form.

The creature let out an unearthly shriek, its form recoiling as if burned by the impromptu blessing. Sabrina's team watched in awe as the shadow began to dissolve, its inky tendrils fading away into nothingness.

As the last traces of the creature disappeared, Sabrina and her team were left standing in the kitchen, their hearts racing and their minds reeling from the encounter. The silence that settled over the room was broken only by the sound of their labored breathing and the distant ticking of the clock on the wall.

Sabrina turned to her team, a triumphant grin spreading across her face. "Well, that was certainly unexpected," she quipped, her voice still shaking slightly from the adrenaline rush. "But I think we can all agree that we make a pretty awesome ghost-busting team."

Mort, and Pepper, exchanged glances, their expressions a mix of relief and admiration for their fearless leader. As they began to clean up the kitchen, Sabrina's thoughts returned to the jukebox and the secrets it held.

Chapter 16

Sabrina slumped at a corner table in the deserted Crossroads Diner, her wavy hair falling into her eyes as she propped her chin on one hand and an untouched mug of coffee sat cold before her.

Through the windows, the late afternoon sun cast long shadows across the checkered linoleum. The empty booths and stools seemed to whisper questions that plagued Sabrina's mind.

"Am I really cut out for this?" Sabrina muttered under her breath. "Talking to ghosts, running a paranormal diner - what was I thinking? Maybe I'm in over my head."

She glanced around at the quirky decor - the vintage posters, the jukebox quietly playing Buddy Holly tunes for phantom listeners. All her efforts to make the diner a supernatural sanctuary suddenly felt childish and naive.

Sabrina's eyes fell on the framed photo behind the counter showing her beaming in front of the diner on opening day last year, an "Under New Management - No Pulse, No Problem!" sign proudly displayed.

"I thought I had it all figured out. That I could help lost souls find closure, give them a place to feel at home." She shook her head ruefully. "But lately, it seems like every ghost has an unsolvable grudge, and I'm just fumbling in the dark."

Her mind flashed to the angry poltergeist who'd sent plates flying last week, the weepy specter she couldn't console, no matter how many spectral tissues she offered. Failure chilled Sabrina more than any ghostly presence.

Spectres and Souffles

Massaging her temples, Sabrina pushed away the cold coffee. Her stomach roiled with ectoplasmic butterflies. "What if I can't protect this place – can't protect them?"

She twisted a lock of hair anxiously around one finger. "There's no Ghost Hostess instruction manual. I'm making this up as I go. And if I mess up, I'm letting down souls with nowhere else to turn. Living and dead."

Sabrina's heart felt heavy as a tombstone. The silence of the empty diner echoed her own spiraling doubts about whether her paranormal Purpose, once so clear, was nothing more than a silly, misguided girl's foolish dream...

As if summoned by her somber thoughts, a familiar figure emerged from the shadows. Mort Grimshaw, the diner's resident reaper, glided towards her table, his black robes billowing behind him like an ethereal cape. The concern etched on his skeletal face was unmistakable, even without the benefit of flesh.

"Why so glum, chum?" Mort asked, his deep voice tinged with worry. "I haven't seen a face that long since the last time I reaped a horse."

Despite her mood, Sabrina couldn't help but crack a smile at Mort's morbid humor. "Oh, you know," she sighed, "just questioning my entire existence and purpose in the grand scheme of things. The usual."

Mort settled into the chair across from her, his bony frame looking almost comical in the plush, retro-style seat. He reached out, his skeletal hand gently touching hers. The cold, smooth bone was strangely comforting, a reminder that death was just another part of the journey.

"Now, listen here, Sabrina," Mort said, his tone uncharacteristically serious. "I've been around the block a few times – heck, I've been around the graveyard more times than I can count – and I know a thing or two about purpose."

Sabrina looked up, meeting Mort's hollow eye sockets. Despite their emptiness, they seemed to hold a wealth of understanding and wisdom.

"You, my dear, have a gift," Mort continued, giving her hand a gentle squeeze. "A gift that allows you to bridge the gap between the living and the dead. Do you have any idea how rare that is? How special?"

Sabrina shrugged, feeling the weight of her doubts lifting ever so slightly. "I guess I never really thought about it like that," she admitted.

"Well, start thinking about it," Mort insisted. "Because let me tell you, in all my eons of reaping, I've never met anyone quite like you. Someone with the power to bring peace to the restless dead and comfort to the grieving living."

As Mort spoke, Sabrina felt a flicker of hope reignite within her. Maybe she wasn't just fumbling in the dark after all. Maybe, just maybe, she was exactly where she was meant to be.

Sabrina took a deep breath, allowing Mort's words to sink in. She glanced around the diner, taking in the eclectic mix of living and ghostly patrons. The air buzzed with the chatter of conversations, both earthly and ethereal, and the clinking of cutlery against plates. It was a symphony of life and afterlife, and she was the conductor.

"You're right," Sabrina said, a smile tugging at the corners of her lips. "I've been so focused on my own doubts that I've forgotten about all the good we've done here."

Mort nodded, his skeletal grin widening. "Exactly! Remember that time we helped that poor, lost soul find his way to the other side? Or when we reunited that ghostly couple who'd been separated for centuries? Those are the moments that matter, Sabrina. Those are the reasons why you're here."

Sabrina's heart swelled with gratitude for Mort's unwavering support. She knew that without him, she would have given up on her paranormal pursuits long ago. But with him by her side, she felt like she could take on anything – even the malevolent spirit of Eliot Blackwood.

As if reading her thoughts, Mort leaned in closer, his voice dropping to a conspiratorial whisper. "Now, about this Eliot fellow. I think it's time we showed him what happens when you mess with the Crossroads Diner and its proprietor."

Sabrina stood up, smoothing down her dress and squaring her shoulders. But as she turned to head towards the kitchen, a sudden commotion erupted from the front of the diner. Startled patrons leaped from their seats as a chilling wind swept through the room, rattling the windows and sending napkins flying.

The lights flickered ominously as Sabrina and Mort raced towards the front of the diner, their footsteps echoing in the eerie silence that had fallen over the once-bustling establishment. Sabrina's heart pounded in her chest, a mixture of fear and determination coursing through her veins.

As they reached the main dining area, Sabrina gasped at the sight before her. There, in the center of the room, stood the ghostly figure of Eliot, his translucent form emanating an aura of malice and despair. His hollow eyes fixed upon Sabrina, a cruel smile twisting his spectral features.

Sabrina steeled herself, refusing to be intimidated by the vengeful spirit. "This diner is a sanctuary for all, and I won't let you destroy that. It's time for you to move on and find peace."

Mort stepped forward, his scythe glinting menacingly in the flickering light.

Eliot threw back his head and laughed, a chilling sound that sent shivers down Sabrina's spine. "You think you can stop me, Reaper? I have grown more powerful than you can possibly imagine. This diner, and all the souls within it, will be mine!"

With a wave of his ghostly hand, Eliot sent a surge of dark energy hurtling towards Sabrina and Mort. They dove out of the way, barely avoiding the crackling blast that scorched the floor where they had been standing moments before.

Sabrina desperately searched for a way to defeat the malevolent spirit. She knew that her unique gift was the key to saving the diner and all those she held dear, but how could she possibly stand against such overwhelming power?

As if sensing her thoughts, Mort reached out and grasped her hand, his bony fingers intertwining with hers. "Remember, Sabrina," he whispered urgently, "you are not alone in this fight. Your friends, both living and dead, stand with you. Draw strength from their love and support, and trust in yourself."

Sabrina nodded, a newfound resolve burning in her eyes. With Mort by her side and the combined power of the spirits she had helped over the years, she knew that she could face anything – even the formidable Eliot Blackwood.

Taking a deep breath, Sabrina stepped forward, her voice ringing out clear and strong. "Eliot, by the power vested in me as the bridge between worlds, I banish you from this realm! May you find the peace in death that eluded you in life!"

As she spoke those words, a brilliant light began to emanate from Sabrina's body, growing brighter and brighter until it filled the entire diner. The spirits of those she had helped over the years appeared beside her, their spectral forms joining their strength to hers.

Eliot screamed in rage and fear as the light engulfed him, his ghostly form slowly dissolving into nothingness. With a final, anguished cry, he vanished, banished from the mortal realm forever.

As the light faded, Sabrina sagged against Mort, exhausted but triumphant. The diner was safe, and the threat of Eliot was no more.

As the diner settled back into its usual rhythm, the spectral customers chattering excitedly about the dramatic banishment they had just witnessed, Sabrina turned to Mort with a grateful smile. "I couldn't have done this without you," she said softly, reaching out to clasp his bony hand in hers. "Your support and guidance have meant everything to me."

Mort's eyes crinkled in a way that Sabrina had come to recognize as a smile. "You give yourself too little credit, my dear," he replied, his voice a comforting rasp. "The strength and determination you showed today have always been within you. I simply helped you to see it."

Sabrina nodded, feeling a warmth spread through her chest at his words.

As if reading her thoughts, Mort gave her hand a gentle squeeze. "The road ahead may be uncertain," he said, "but I have no doubt that you will continue to be a beacon of hope for the lost souls who find their way to your door."

Sabrina's smile widened, and she felt a renewed sense of purpose suffuse her being. She knew that her gift was a rare and precious thing, and she was determined to use it to make a difference in the lives of both the living and the dead.

Sabrina felt a sense of peace settle over her. For now, at least, all was right in her world.

Sabrina clenched her fists on the table. The doubts that had plagued her mind moments ago dissolved like morning mist, replaced by an unshakable resolve. She knew what she had to do.

"Mort, I can't let Eliot threaten everything we've built here. It's more than just a restaurant - it's a sanctuary for lost souls, both living and dead." Sabrina's voice was steady, infused with a newfound strength. "I have to confront him and protect what's ours."

Mort's skeletal grin widened, the ethereal light in his eyes dancing with pride. He rose from his seat, the folds of his black robes swishing softly. Reaching out a bony hand, he rested it gently on Sabrina's shoulder, the weight of his support tangible despite his spectral form.

"And I'll be right there with you, every step of the way," Mort assured her, his otherworldly voice resonating with unwavering loyalty. "We've faced tougher challenges than a disgruntled dishwasher with a chip on his shoulder. Together, we'll send Eliot packing faster than a ghost with a hot date in the afterlife."

Sabrina couldn't help but chuckle at Mort's morbid wit, the tension in her shoulders easing slightly. She stood up, squaring her shoulders as if preparing for battle. The vintage floral print of her dress seemed to take on a more vibrant hue, mirroring the fire in her eyes.

"Let's do this," Sabrina declared, her voice ringing with conviction. She strode towards the kitchen with purposeful steps, Mort gliding silently beside her. The air crackled with an otherworldly energy as the duo prepared to face the malevolent force threatening their beloved diner.

Little did they know, Eliot was watching from the shadows with malicious intent. As Sabrina and Mort disappeared into the kitchen, he melted back into the darkness, a sinister smile playing on his lips. The stage was set for a showdown.

Sabrina burst into the kitchen scanning the room for her loyal staff. The scent of freshly baked apple pie mingled with the tang of supernatural energy, creating an oddly comforting aroma. Pots and pans clattered as ghostly line cooks hustled to prepare orders, their translucent forms shimmering under the fluorescent lights.

"Listen up, everyone!" Sabrina called out, her voice cutting through the chaos. "We've got a situation on our hands. Eliot, our not-so-friendly neighborhood dishwasher, has gone rogue. We need to confront him and protect our diner from whatever mischief he's planning."

The spectral staff exchanged worried glances, their whispers echoing like the rustle of autumn leaves. Sabrina felt a flicker of doubt, wondering if she was leading her team into danger. But as Mort's reassuring presence loomed beside her, she pushed those thoughts aside.

"I know we've faced our fair share of supernatural shenanigans," Sabrina continued, her tone growing more confident with each word. "But this is our home, our sanctuary. We can't let Eliot destroy everything we've built here. Are you with me?"

A resounding chorus of "Ayes!" filled the kitchen, accompanied by the clatter of spectral utensils. Sabrina felt a surge of pride as she looked around at her dedicated team, each one ready to stand by her side in the face of adversity.

As the ghostly staff rallied around Sabrina, Mort watched from the doorway, his skeletal grin widening with admiration. He had seen countless souls pass through the veil, but none quite like Sabrina. Her unwavering determination and loyalty to her otherworldly patrons was a rare sight, even for a seasoned reaper like himself.

"Alright, team," Sabrina said, her eyes sparkling with mischief. "Let's show Eliot what happens when you mess with the Crossroads Diner. We'll hit him with everything we've got - from ectoplasmic spatulas to ghostly frying pans. He won't know what hit him!"

The kitchen erupted in a flurry of activity as the spectral staff armed themselves with an array of supernatural cooking utensils. Sabrina grabbed a glowing ladle, its ethereal light casting an eerie glow across her features. She turned to Mort, a wry smile playing on her lips.

"Ready to give Eliot a taste of his own medicine?" she asked, twirling the ladle like a baton.

Mort chuckled, the sound echoing through the kitchen like the toll of a distant bell. "Oh, I've got a feeling this is going to be a dish best served cold," he quipped, his scythe gleaming with anticipation.

With a determined nod, Sabrina led her team out of the kitchen, ready to confront the malevolent force threatening their beloved diner. The air crackled with supernatural energy as they marched towards the dining room, their footsteps echoing like the beat of a ghostly drum.

Little did they know, Eliot was waiting for them, his malicious intentions coiled like a snake ready to strike. The final showdown was about to begin, and the fate of the Crossroads Diner hung in the balance.

As Sabrina and her motley crew of supernatural allies burst through the kitchen doors, the once bustling diner fell silent. The air grew thick with tension, the only sound the distant ticking of the vintage clock on the wall. Eliot stood in the center of the room, his dark eyes fixed on Sabrina, a sinister smile playing on his lips.

"Well, well, well," he drawled, his voice dripping with malice. "If it isn't the little ghost whisperer and her band of misfits. I must say, I'm impressed you've managed to keep this place afloat for so long."

Sabrina's grip tightened on her glowing ladle, the ethereal light casting shadows across her face. "Eliot," she said, her voice steady despite the fear churning in her gut. "We know what you're up to, and we won't let you succeed."

Eliot threw his head back and laughed, the sound sending chills down Sabrina's spine. "Oh, you foolish girl," he sneered. "You have no idea what you're up against. I've been planning this for years, and I won't let a bunch of second-rate specters stand in my way."

François stepped forward, his ghostly form shimmering with anger. "You underestimate us, monsieur," he said, his French accent thick with disdain. "We may be dead, but we still have a few tricks up our sleeves."

Pepper nodded, her fiery hair billowing around her face as she raised her wand. "That's right," she said, her voice trembling with determination. "We're not going down without a fight."

Eliot's eyes narrowed, his gaze darting between the members of Sabrina's team. "Very well," he said, his voice low and menacing. "If it's a fight you want, it's a fight you shall have."

With a flick of his wrist, Eliot sent a blast of dark energy hurtling towards them. Sabrina dove out of the way, her heart pounding in her chest as she rolled to her feet. The battle had begun, and the fate of the Crossroads Diner hung in the balance.

Boo let out a ghostly howl, his ethereal form charging towards Eliot, teeth bared. Mort swung his scythe, the blade slicing through the air with a haunting whistle. Pepper fired off a barrage of spells, the colorful bolts of magic ricocheting off the walls.

Sabrina joined the fray, her ladle glowing brighter with each passing second. She swung it like a sword, the ethereal light cutting through the darkness like a beacon of hope. The diner erupted into chaos, tables overturning and glasses shattering as the battle raged on.

But Eliot was a formidable foe, his dark magic seeming to absorb their attacks like a black hole. He laughed maniacally, his eyes glinting with malevolent glee. "Is that all you've got?" he taunted, his voice booming over the din of battle.

Sabrina gritted her teeth, her mind racing as she tried to think of a way to turn the tide. She glanced around the diner, her eyes falling on the vintage jukebox in the corner. A sudden idea struck her, and she turned to her team, her voice urgent.

"The jukebox!" she shouted, pointing towards the glowing machine. "We need to channel our energy into it, create a feedback loop that will overload his magic!"

Mort nodded, his skeletal face grim with determination. "It's worth a shot," he said, his scythe at the ready. "Let's do this."

As one, Sabrina and her team focused their supernatural energy on the jukebox, the machine beginning to hum and crackle with power. Eliot's eyes widened in realization, but it was too late.

The jukebox exploded with a burst of blinding light, the force of the blast sending Eliot flying backwards. He hit the wall with a sickening thud, his dark magic dissipating like smoke in the wind.

Sabrina stood tall, her ladle still glowing with ethereal might. She strode forward, her eyes locked on Eliot's crumpled form. She had done it. She had protected her diner, her team, and the countless souls that called this place home.

But as she drew closer, she realized something was amiss. Eliot's body was no longer there, only a scorch mark on the wall where he had fallen. A chill ran down her spine as a sudden realization hit her.

This wasn't over.

Chapter 17

The spectral kitchen crackled with an eerie energy as Sabrina stormed in, her dress swishing angrily around her legs. The normally warm expression that greeted customers with a twinkle now blazed fiercely as they locked onto Eliot's lean form. He stood at the sink, methodically scrubbing a dish, his back to her.

"Eliot," Sabrina demanded, her usually chipper voice edged with steel. "We need to talk. Now."

Eliot slowly set the dish down and turned to face her, a sly smirk playing at the corner of his mouth. As he moved, his form shimmered and shifted, like heat waves rising off summer asphalt. Sabrina blinked, momentarily taken aback by the display of his shapeshifting abilities.

So it's true, she thought grimly. *He's not just a dishwasher with a mysterious past. He's one of them.*

"Sabrina," Eliot drawled, stretching out the syllables of her name. "To what do I owe the pleasure?"

"Cut the crap, Eliot. I know about your involvement in François's death. How could you betray us like this? The Crossroads Diner was your home!"

Eliot let out a dark chuckle, the sound sending chills down Sabrina's spine despite the warmth of the kitchen. "Betray you? Oh, my dear Sabrina, you have no idea."

He began to pace, his form flickering between human and something far more sinister. "I've harbored a grudge against the culinary world for far too long. The pretentious chefs, the snooty critics, the fickle foodies - they all disgust me."

Sabrina's heart raced as she listened, a sinking feeling growing in her gut. She had always sensed there was more to Eliot than met the eye, but this?

"And your precious little diner," Eliot sneered, "with its quaint charm and humble menu? It's the perfect target. I'm going to transform it into the most pretentious bistro this town has ever seen. Molecular gastronomy, deconstructed dishes, obscure ingredients - the works. And I'll erase every trace of its humble origins."

Rage boiled up inside Sabrina, mixing with the bitter sting of betrayal. She clenched her fists at her sides, nails digging into her palms. "I won't let you do this, Eliot. The Crossroads Diner means everything to me, to the community - both living and dead. I'll fight you with every fiber of my being."

Eliot threw his head back and laughed, the sound bouncing off the stainless steel surfaces. "Oh, I'm counting on it, Sabrina. In fact, I'm looking forward to it."

With a final, unsettling grin, Eliot vanished, his form dissipating into wisps of shadow. Sabrina stood alone in the spectral kitchen, her heart hammering in her chest, the gravity of the situation crashing down on her.

Sabrina stood her ground, the spectral kitchen pulsing with an eerie energy. She locked eyes with Eliot, her voice steady and unwavering. "You underestimate the strength of this community, Eliot. We've faced challenges before, and we've always come out stronger. Your malevolent intentions won't destroy what we've built here."

Eliot's lips curled into a mocking smile. "Ah, Sabrina, ever the optimist. But you have no idea what you're up against." He began to pace, shadows swirling around his feet like obedient pets. "I've spent years perfecting my craft, honing my abilities. And now, I'm going to use them to tear down everything you hold dear."

Sabrina's heart raced, but she refused to let fear take hold. As if sensing her thoughts, Eliot's eyes glinted with malice. "Let me give you a taste of what's to come, Sabrina." With a flick of his wrist, the kitchen plunged into darkness, shadows swirling and twisting like malevolent entities.

Sabrina gasped as the shadows closed in on her, their icy tendrils brushing against her skin. Spectral illusions danced before her eyes— visions of the diner in ruins, its once-vibrant walls crumbling, its loyal patrons scattered to the winds.

Spectres and Souffles

No! Sabrina screamed, fighting against the onslaught of despair. She closed her eyes, focusing on the love and warmth that had always been the heart of the Crossroads Diner. The laughter of satisfied customers, the sizzle of burgers on the grill, the camaraderie of her ghostly regulars—those were the things that truly mattered.

With a burst of determination, Sabrina opened her eyes, her gaze cutting through the shadows. "Your illusions have no power over me, Eliot. I know what's real, and I know what I'm fighting for."

Eliot's face contorted with fury, the shadows around him writhing like angry serpents. "We'll see about that, Sabrina. We'll see just how long your resolve can last in the face of true darkness."

The air crackled with tension, the spectral kitchen transformed into a battleground of wills. Sabrina stood tall, her love for the Crossroads Diner and its community burning bright within her. She knew the fight ahead would be difficult, but she was ready to face whatever challenges Eliot threw her way.

Just as the shadows threatened to engulf Sabrina, a brilliant, ethereal light pierced through the darkness. The ghostly form of François materialized beside her, his presence radiating a sense of warmth and resolve. Sabrina's eyes widened in surprise, a flicker of hope igniting within her.

"François?" she whispered, her voice trembling with a mix of relief and disbelief.

The spectral chef turned to Sabrina, his translucent features softened by a gentle smile. "I've been watching, Sabrina. I've seen your unwavering dedication to the Crossroads Diner and the paranormal community. Your strength and love have touched my soul."

Eliot's eyes narrowed, his shadowy aura pulsing with anger. "Well, well, if it isn't the ghost of chefs past. Come to join the losing side, François?"

François' gaze hardened as he faced Eliot, his ghostly form shimmering with determination. "I'm here to remind you of what truly matters, Eliot. The culinary arts are about bringing joy and comfort to others, not about petty grudges and selfish ambitions."

Sabrina felt a surge of strength coursing through her, bolstered by François' unexpected support. She stepped forward, standing shoulder to shoulder with the ghostly chef. "François is right, Eliot. Your actions threaten to destroy the very essence of what makes the Crossroads Diner special."

Eliot scoffed, his shapeshifting form rippling with malice. "Special? It's nothing more than a rundown relic, a reminder of a bygone era. I'm here to elevate it, to make it something truly exceptional."

François shook his head, his voice filled with a quiet intensity. "You're mistaken, Eliot. The Crossroads Diner is already exceptional. It's a place where the living and the dead can find solace, where the simple act of sharing a meal can bridge the gap between worlds."

As François spoke, the spectral kitchen began to shift, the shadows receding ever so slightly.

Sabrina closed her eyes, reaching out with her mind to connect with François's spectral essence. She visualized the threads that bound them together, the shared love for the diner and the culinary arts that had forged their unlikely friendship.

But as she stretched out her senses, she encountered an unexpected void. The familiar warmth of François's presence was absent, replaced by a chilling emptiness that sent a shiver down her spine.

"François?" Sabrina called out, her voice trembling slightly. "I can't feel you. What's happening?"

The ghostly chef's form flickered, his edges blurring as if he were being pulled away by an unseen force. François looked at Sabrina, his eyes wide with confusion and a hint of fear.

"I... I don't know," he admitted, his voice sounding distant and strained. "It's as if something is blocking our connection, severing the bond we share."

Eliot's laughter echoed through the spectral kitchen, a cruel and mocking sound that set Sabrina's teeth on edge. "Poor little Sabrina," he taunted, his shapeshifting form swirling with malevolent energy. "It seems your precious ghost whisperer abilities have failed you when you need them most."

She looked at François, desperately seeking reassurance, but the ghostly chef's form continued to flicker, his presence growing weaker with each passing moment.

The air in the spectral kitchen grew heavy with tension, the shadows swirling around them like a gathering storm. Sabrina knew she had to act fast, to find a way to break through the barrier blocking her connection with François before it was too late.

She took a deep breath, centering herself amidst the chaos. Sabrina focused her energy, reaching out once more to François, her mind grasping for any flicker of their bond that remained. The fate of the diner hung in the balance, and she refused to let it slip through her fingers.

As Sabrina struggled to reconnect with François, Mort, Pepper, and Boo emerged from the shadows, their faces etched with concern. They gathered around Sabrina, their presence a comforting balm amidst the turmoil.

"Sabrina, my dear," Mort said, his voice a soothing whisper, "do not let Eliot's words poison your resolve. You are stronger than you know, and we are here to support you."

Pepper nodded, her fiery hair dancing with determination. "Mort's right, Sabrina. You've faced tougher challenges before, and you've always come out on top. Don't forget that."

Boo let out a soft bark, his ethereal tail wagging in encouragement. Even without words, his message was clear: *We believe in you, Sabrina.*

Sabrina felt a flicker of warmth in her chest, the love and support of her friends reigniting the embers of her courage. She looked at each of them, a grateful smile tugging at her lips.

"Thank you," she said, her voice steady despite the weight of the moment. "I don't know what I'd do without you all."

Mort placed a bony hand on Sabrina's shoulder, his touch surprisingly gentle for a being of death. "You are never alone, Sabrina."

Sabrina took a deep breath, the scent of spectral energy and determination filling her lungs. She closed her eyes, focusing her mind and heart on the task at hand.

As Sabrina opened her eyes. She locked gazes with Eliot, her voice steady and unwavering.

"You may have blocked my connection with François, Eliot, but you underestimate the power of the Crossroads Diner and the strength of our bond. I will find a way to overcome this, and when I do, you'll wish you never set foot in my kitchen."

Eliot's smirk faltered for a moment, a flicker of uncertainty crossing his face. Sabrina's anger was palpable, a force to be reckoned with. Sabrina's hands glowed with an ethereal light as she channeled her energy, ready to unleash her unique abilities upon Eliot. Mort, Pepper, and Boo stood beside her, their own powers at the ready.

Mort's skeletal grin widened as he summoned a swirling vortex of ghostly energy. "I've been waiting for this moment," he quipped, his eye sockets gleaming with mischief. "Time to send this shapeshifter back to the spectral doghouse!"

Pepper's tattoos pulsed with magical energy, her fiery hair whipping around her face as she prepared to unleash a barrage of spells. "I've got a few explosive surprises up my sleeve," she grinned, her eyes sparkling with excitement. "Eliot won't know what hit him!"

Boo let out a fierce bark, his ethereal form shimmering as he channeled his intuitive abilities to sense Eliot's weaknesses.

The battle erupted in a dazzling display of supernatural power. Sabrina's spectral energy collided with Eliot's dark magic, the air crackling with intensity. Mort's ghostly vortex swirled around the shapeshifter, disorienting him and weakening his hold on the spectral kitchen.

Pepper's spells exploded in bursts of vibrant color, her unpredictable magic keeping Eliot on his toes. Boo darted between the combatants, his timely barks and warnings guiding his friends as they fought against the malevolent force.

As the battle reached its climax, Sabrina felt a surge of energy building within her. She locked eyes with her teammates, a silent understanding passing between them. It was now or never.

"Everyone, focus your energy on me!" Sabrina shouted, her voice rising above the chaos. "We'll combine our powers and break free from Eliot's grasp!"

Mort, Pepper, and Boo nodded in unison, their faces set with determination. They channeled their unique abilities, directing their energy towards Sabrina in a brilliant convergence of supernatural power.

Spectres and Souffles

The air hummed with electricity as Sabrina absorbed the combined energy of her team. She felt it coursing through her veins, a tingling sensation that grew in intensity with each passing second.

With a fierce cry, Sabrina unleashed the concentrated energy towards Eliot in a blinding burst of light. The shapeshifter's eyes widened in surprise as the surge of power slammed into him, weakening his hold on the spectral kitchen.

The team seized the opportunity, breaking free from Eliot's grasp and surrounding him in a circle of determined faces. They stood tall, their powers at the ready, prepared to confront the malevolent force head-on.

"It's over, Eliot," Sabrina declared, her voice ringing with authority. "You've underestimated the strength of the Crossroads Diner and the bond we share. Now, it's time for you to face the consequences of your actions."

Eliot's eyes narrowed, his form flickering between shadows as he fought to maintain control. "You think you can defeat me?" he sneered, his voice echoing through the spectral kitchen. "I've been planning this for ages, Sabrina. Your little diner and your motley crew are no match for my power."

Sabrina stood her ground, unflinching in the face of Eliot's taunts.

"You're wrong, Eliot," Sabrina countered, her voice steady and determined. "This diner is more than just a place. It's a sanctuary, a home for those who have nowhere else to go."

Eliot's eyes widened in disbelief as Sabrina began to glow, her form radiating with an otherworldly light. The spirits of the diner swirled around her, their whispers of encouragement filling the air. Mort, Pepper, and Boo stood beside her, their own powers intertwining with hers in a dazzling display of unity.

With a final, triumphant cry, Sabrina unleashed the full force of her power, directing it towards Eliot in a blinding burst of energy. The shapeshifter's form began to dissipate, his malevolent presence unraveling under the onslaught of Sabrina's resolve.

"No!" Eliot screamed, his voice fading into the ether. "This can't be happening!"

But it was too late. The combined strength of Sabrina, her team, and the spirits of the Crossroads Diner proved too much for Eliot to withstand. With a final, anguished howl, his form shattered into a million spectral fragments, scattering to the far reaches of the otherworld.

As the last traces of Eliot's presence vanished, the spectral kitchen fell silent. Sabrina, her chest heaving with exertion, turned to face her team. Mort, Pepper, and Boo looked back at her, their faces etched with a mix of relief and awe.

"We did it," Sabrina whispered, a tired smile tugging at the corners of her lips. "We saved the diner."

Sabrina stumbled forward, her legs trembling from the exertion of channeling such immense power. Mort, ever the attentive friend, materialized by her side, his skeletal arm offering support. "Easy there, boss," he quipped, his ethereal voice tinged with concern. "That was one hell of a light show you put on."

Pepper, her fiery hair disheveled from the battle, bounded over to Sabrina, her eyes wide with excitement. "That was incredible, Sabrina! I mean, I've seen some impressive spellwork in my day, but you? You were like a supernova of supernatural energy!"

Boo, the loyal canine ghost, nuzzled against Sabrina's leg, his translucent tail wagging in a gesture of comfort and reassurance. Sabrina reached down, her fingers passing through Boo's ethereal fur, and smiled. "Thanks, guys. I couldn't have done it without you."

As the team stood amidst the remnants of the spectral kitchen, the weight of their victory slowly sank in. The tantalizing aromas of ghostly delicacies mingled with the lingering scent of Eliot's defeat, creating a peculiar bouquet that tickled their noses.

Sabrina's gaze swept across the room, taking in the chaos that had unfolded. Shattered plates and scattered utensils littered the floor, a testament to the intensity of their battle. Yet, amidst the disarray, she couldn't help but feel a sense of pride. They had faced an insurmountable challenge and emerged victorious, their bonds stronger than ever.

"So, what now?" Mort asked, his glowing eye sockets fixated on Sabrina. "Do we celebrate with a spectral soirée? I hear François makes a mean ghostly goulash."

Sabrina chuckled, shaking her head. "As tempting as that sounds, I think we have some cleaning up to do first. The Crossroads Diner has seen better days."

Spectres and Souffles

Pepper, her enthusiasm undiminished, clapped her hands together. "No worries! With a little magical elbow grease and some supernatural teamwork, we'll have this place spick and span in no time!"

As the last of the ghostly dishes clinked into place, Sabrina turned to her team, a mischievous glint in her eye. "Alright, gang. Who's up for a little celebratory haunted house hunting? I hear there's a new specter in town that's been causing quite a stir."

Mort, Pepper, exchanged knowing grins, their eagerness palpable. With a collective nod, they gathered around Sabrina, ready to embark on their next otherworldly adventure.

Chapter 18

Sabrina slumped against the wall, her dress torn and singed, as she surveyed the wreckage of the Crossroads Diner. Shards of glass and splinters of wood littered the black and white checkered floor. The jukebox lay on its side, vinyl records spilled out like disemboweled organs.

"Everyone still in one piece? More or less?" Sabrina called out, wincing as she prodded a purpling bruise on her arm. Soft groans answered her from behind overturned tables.

"I think my spleen is in my sock, but otherwise I'm peachy," Mort deadpanned, his ghostly form flickering as he floated up from behind the counter.

Pepper's red beehive hairdo poked up next. "Honey, I've had rougher nights after one too many martinis. But yeah, we're still kickin'. Figuratively speaking."

Sabrina couldn't help but chuckle, even as every muscle protested the movement. Leave it to her band of misfit spirits to find the dark humor in narrowly surviving the apocalypse. Again.

She took a deep breath, the familiar smells of coffee and pie mingling with the acrid stench of brimstone. Time to pick up the pieces. "Alrighty gang, let's get this place cleaned up. I have a feeling we're going to have some shell-shocked customers looking for a safe haven."

As if on cue, the battered front door creaked open. A bedraggled werewolf and a vampire missing half an eyebrow peered inside hesitantly.

"Come on in, boys," Sabrina called, her most welcoming smile firmly in place despite the fact that her hair probably resembled a tumbleweed. "The coffee's on and the pie's...well, the pie might be a bit crunchy today, but it's still edible. Probably."

The werewolf's tail gave a tentative wag as he slunk inside, the vampire following suit. Within minutes, the clinking of mugs and the low murmur of conversation filled the air as more patrons, both living and deceased, sought out the sanctuary of the Crossroads.

Sabrina surveyed her domain, warmth blossoming in her chest. The diner might be a little worse for wear, but it was still standing. Still a beacon of hope and camaraderie in the often chaotic world of the paranormal.

She caught Mort's eye as he righted a chair, his wink saying more than words ever could. They'd been through Hell together, quite literally, and come out the other side. Stranger things might be lurking in the shadows, but for now, in this moment, all was well.

Sabrina rolled up her sleeves, ignoring the ache in her muscles. "Alright everybody, who ordered the supernatural special with a side of wry?" The answering chuckles were music to her ears as she headed back into the fray, ready to face whatever the next chapter might bring.

Sabrina grinned as she expertly balanced a tray laden with steaming mugs and plates, navigating the bustling diner with practiced ease. She paused at Mort's table, where he sat with Pepper and Boo, the unlikely trio engrossed in a lively debate.

"All I'm saying," Pepper gestured with a french fry, "is that if we're going to be battling interdimensional beasties on the regular, we should at least get some sort of frequent flyer miles."

Mort snorted, his skeletal fingers wrapped around a mug of black coffee. "And what, pray tell, would you do with said miles? Take a vacation to the seventh circle?"

"Hey, I hear they have great lava pools this time of year," Pepper quipped, popping the fry into her mouth with a grin.

Boo let out a bark that sounded suspiciously like a laugh, his ghostly tail wagging in amusement.

Sabrina chuckled, setting down their orders with a flourish. "Well, if we're going to start a rewards program, we should probably come up with a catchy name. 'Paranormal Perks'? 'Specter Savings'?"

"'Ghoul's Gold'?" Mort suggested, his eyes glinting with mirth.

The banter continued, the easy camaraderie a balm to Sabrina's weary soul. These were her people, her family. They'd been through thick and thin together, and she wouldn't trade them for the world.

As the conversation lulled, Sabrina's gaze drifted to Ambrose, who sat alone at the counter, his brow furrowed as he stared into his coffee. Her heart clenched, a mix of longing and uncertainty swirling in her gut.

Excusing herself from the table, Sabrina made her way over to him, sliding onto the stool beside him. "Penny for your thoughts?" she asked softly, studying his profile.

Ambrose glanced up, a wry smile tugging at his lips. "I'm not sure they're worth that much, to be honest."

Sabrina reached out, her hand hovering over his for a moment before she let it rest on the cool Formica of the counter. "Ambrose, about...about us..."

He turned to face her fully, his blue eyes searching her face. "Sabrina, I know things have been...complicated, to say the least. But I need you to know that my feelings for you, they're real. They've always been real."

Sabrina bit her lip, her heart racing. "But how can I be sure? With everything that's happened, everything we've been through..."

Ambrose took her hand, his touch warm and reassuring. "I know I've given you reason to doubt me, and for that, I'm truly sorry. But I'm here now, and I'm not going anywhere. Not unless you tell me to."

Sabrina swallowed past the lump in her throat, her eyes stinging with unshed tears. "I don't want you to go," she whispered, her voice raw with emotion. "But I'm scared, Ambrose. Scared of getting hurt again."

He squeezed her hand, his gaze never wavering. "I can't promise that things will always be easy, but I can promise that I will always be honest with you. That I will always fight for you, for us."

Sabrina nodded, a tentative smile curving her lips. "I want to believe that, more than anything."

"Then let me prove it to you," Ambrose murmured, his thumb brushing over her knuckles. "One day at a time, one moment at a time. Let me show you that what we have is worth fighting for."

Sabrina's heart swelled, hope blossoming in her chest. "Okay," she breathed, her smile widening. "Okay, let's give this a shot."

Ambrose grinned, his eyes sparkling with joy and relief. He raised her hand to his lips, pressing a gentle kiss to her fingers. "You won't regret this, Sabrina. I promise."

Spectres and Souffles

And for the first time in a long time, Sabrina believed him. Believed in them. Whatever the future held, they would face it together. One supernatural crisis at a time.

Sabrina stepped into the bustling Crossroads Diner, the familiar chatter of patrons and the clink of silverware filling the air. Her gaze swept over the room, taking in the lively mix of living and deceased customers. Ambrose followed close behind, his presence a reassuring warmth at her back.

As they navigated the crowded space, Sabrina couldn't help but marvel at the way Ambrose seamlessly integrated himself into the diner's daily routine. He flashed a charming smile at a group of elderly ghosts, who tittered and waved in response, before gracefully sidestepping a harried waitress balancing a tray laden with steaming plates.

"Impressive footwork," Sabrina teased, shooting him a playful grin over her shoulder. "You're a natural."

Ambrose chuckled, his eyes crinkling at the corners. "I learned from the best," he quipped, inclining his head towards her.

As they reached the counter, Sabrina was greeted by the sight of Mort, Pepper, and Boo huddled together, engaged in a lively discussion. Their faces lit up as they spotted her, and Boo let out an enthusiastic bark.

Ambrose dipped into a theatrical bow, eliciting a round of laughter from the trio. "At your service," he declared, his eyes twinkling with mirth.

Sabrina's heart swelled as she watched Ambrose effortlessly integrate himself into her found family. He listened attentively as Mort regaled him with tales of his glory days, nodded sympathetically as Pepper lamented the challenges of managing unruly spirit patrons.

"He's a keeper," Pepper murmured, sidling up to Sabrina and nudging her playfully. "I haven't seen you smile like that in ages."

Sabrina ducked her head, feeling a blush creep up her cheeks. "It's still early days," she demurred, but the warmth in her voice betrayed her growing affection for the enigmatic food critic.

As the day wore on, Sabrina found herself marveling at Ambrose's genuine commitment to the diner and its eclectic clientele. He approached each task with enthusiasm and care, whether it was brewing the perfect cup of ghostly Earl Grey or lending a sympathetic ear to a troubled spirit.

"You're a natural at this," Sabrina mused, watching as Ambrose deftly navigated a conversation with a particularly cantankerous ghost. "It's like you've been doing this all your life."

Ambrose shrugged, a small smile tugging at the corners of his mouth. "I've always been drawn to the unconventional," he admitted, his gaze drifting to meet hers. "And there's something about this place, about you, that just feels right."

Sabrina's heart skipped a beat, and she found herself reaching out to take his hand, twining their fingers together. "I'm glad you're here," she murmured, her voice soft but sincere.

As the sun began to set and the diner's neon sign flickered to life, Sabrina took a moment to survey the scene before her. The Crossroads Diner was alive with laughter and chatter, the living and the dead mingling together in a harmonious tapestry. And at the center of it all was Ambrose, his presence a steady anchor in the midst of the supernatural chaos.

Sabrina's reverie was interrupted by the sudden appearance of a familiar ghostly figure. Old Man Jenkins, a regular at the Crossroads Diner, glided through the wall, his translucent form shimmering in the neon light. He made a beeline for his usual booth, settling in with a contented sigh.

"Evening, Jenkins!" Sabrina called out, a warm smile spreading across her face. "The usual?"

The elderly spirit nodded, his wispy beard bobbing with the motion. "You know me too well, Sabrina. A spectral special, if you please."

With a chuckle, Sabrina made her way to the kitchen, her mind already whirring with the ingredients she'd need to whip up Jenkins' favorite dish. As she worked, her thoughts drifted to the challenges they'd faced in the recent past. The showdown with the malevolent entity had tested them all, pushing them to their limits and forcing them to confront their deepest fears.

But in the end, they'd emerged stronger, their bonds forged in the fires of adversity. Sabrina glanced over at Mort, who was regaling a group of wide-eyed patrons with tales of his ghostly exploits. Pepper flitted

Spectres and Souffles

from table to table, her infectious laughter filling the air, while Boo kept a watchful eye on the proceedings, ever the vigilant guardian.

And then there was Ambrose. Sabrina's heart swelled with gratitude as she watched him move through the diner, his easy charm and quick wit putting even the most restless spirits at ease. He'd proven himself time and again, not just as a valuable member of the team, but as a true friend and confidant.

As she plated Jenkins' spectral special, Sabrina felt a renewed sense of purpose and determination. The Crossroads Diner was more than just a restaurant; it was a haven, a place where the living and the dead could come together in a spirit of unity and understanding. And she, Sabrina Spellsworth, was the bridge between those two worlds.

With a flourish, she delivered the dish to Jenkins' table, his ghostly eyes lighting up with delight. "You're a treasure, Sabrina," he declared, digging in with gusto.

Sabrina grinned, her eyes sparkling with mischief. "Careful there, Jenkins. Flattery like that might just go to my head."

As she turned to head back to the kitchen, Sabrina paused, taking in the scene before her. The Crossroads Diner was a tapestry of life and death, a place where the boundaries between worlds blurred and the impossible became everyday occurrence. And at the heart of it all was a quirky, quick-witted woman with a heart as big as the great beyond.

Sabrina Spellsworth, paranormal proprietor extraordinaire, was right where she belonged. And she couldn't wait to see what ghostly adventures the future had in store.

Sabrina's attention was drawn to a quiet corner of the diner, where a translucent elderly woman sat alone, her shoulders slumped and her eyes downcast. Recognizing the signs of a troubled spirit, Sabrina made her way over, a warm smile on her face.

"Hey there, sugar," she greeted, sliding into the booth across from the woman. "I'm Sabrina. Can I get you anything? A cup of coffee, perhaps? Or maybe one of our famous ectoplasmic éclairs?"

The woman looked up, her ghostly features etched with sadness. "Oh, no thank you, dear. I'm afraid I don't have much of an appetite these days."

Sabrina reached out, her hand hovering just above the woman's translucent one. "Want to talk about it? I've been told I'm a pretty good listener, and I've got a knack for helping folks sort through their otherworldly woes."

The woman hesitated for a moment, then sighed. "It's my grandson, you see. He's been having a tough time since I passed, and I worry about him constantly. I just wish there was some way I could let him know that I'm still here, watching over him."

Sabrina nodded, her eyes filled with compassion. "I understand completely. It's hard, being separated from the ones we love. But you know what? I bet we can find a way to get a message to your grandson. Between you and me, I've got a few tricks up my sleeve when it comes to bridging the gap between the living and the dead."

The woman's face brightened, a glimmer of hope in her ghostly eyes. "You really think so?"

"I know so," Sabrina assured her, a mischievous twinkle in her eye. "Now, let's put our heads together and come up with a plan. I'm thinking a ghostly greeting card, delivered by yours truly. What do you say?"

As Sabrina and the woman huddled together, conspiring and chuckling, the rest of the Crossroads Diner hummed with activity. Mort, Pepper, and Boo moved effortlessly between tables, taking orders and serving up dishes with a side of good-natured banter.

"Order up!" Mort called from the kitchen, sliding a plate of sizzling spectral sliders through the pass-through. "One 'Haunted Hamburger Platter,' extra pickles, hold the ectoplasm."

Pepper snagged the plate, balancing it expertly on her tray. "You got it, boss. And might I say, your alliteration is on point today."

Boo, meanwhile, was engaged in a lively debate with a table of ghostly philosophers, his quick wit and clever quips keeping them on their toes. "All I'm saying is, if a tree falls in the forest and no one's around to hear it, does it make a sound? And more importantly, does it leave a ghost?"

The philosophers roared with laughter, their spectral forms shimmering with mirth. "Boo, my boy," one of them chuckled, "you never fail to bring a fresh perspective to the eternal questions."

Spectres and Souffles

As Sabrina watched her team in action, she couldn't help but feel a swell of pride. The Crossroads Diner was more than just a restaurant; it was a community, a place where the living and the dead could come together to share stories, laughter, and the occasional existential crisis.

And at the heart of it all was a quirky, quick-witted woman with a heart as big as the great beyond, and a talent for making the impossible seem like just another day at the office.

Sabrina's reverie was interrupted by the jingle of the bell above the door, heralding the arrival of a familiar face. Ambrose Saffron, the enigmatic food critic, stepped into the diner, his tailored suit and polished shoes a stark contrast to the vintage decor.

"Ambrose!" Sabrina greeted him with a warm smile, a flutter of excitement in her chest. "What brings you to our little corner of the cosmos today?"

He returned her smile, his blue eyes twinkling with mischief. "I heard a rumor that the Crossroads Diner is serving up the best 'Spectral Soufflé' this side of the veil. I couldn't resist the temptation to taste it for myself."

Sabrina laughed, gesturing for him to take a seat at the counter. "Well, you're in luck. I just whipped up a fresh batch this morning. Prepare to have your taste buds haunted in the best way possible."

As she served him a generous portion of the ethereal dessert, Ambrose leaned in, his voice lowering conspiratorially. "I must admit, Sabrina, your culinary creations are only part of the reason I keep coming back. The company is equally enchanting."

Sabrina felt a blush creep up her cheeks, but she met his gaze with a playful smirk. "Careful, Ambrose. Flattery like that might earn you an extra scoop of 'Ghostly Ganache.'"

They settled into a comfortable banter, trading stories and jokes as Ambrose savored every bite of the 'Spectral Soufflé.' Sabrina found herself drawn to his wit and charm, the connection between them growing stronger with each shared laugh.

He's not just a food critic, she mused silently, watching him gesture animatedly as he recounted a particularly humorous anecdote. *He's a kindred spirit, someone who appreciates the magic and mystery of this place.*

As the hours slipped by and the diner began to empty, Sabrina and Ambrose lingered, lost in conversation. The warmth of his presence filled her with a sense of contentment, a feeling that, despite the chaos and challenges of her unusual life, she was exactly where she was meant to be.

Finally, Ambrose glanced at his watch, a rueful smile on his lips. "As much as I'd love to stay and unravel the secrets of the universe with you, Sabrina, I'm afraid I have a prior engagement with a particularly persnickety poltergeist."

Sabrina walked him to the door, her hand brushing against his as they said their goodbyes. "Until next time, then. Don't be a stranger, Ambrose. The 'Spectral Soufflé' will be waiting for you."

As the door closed behind him, Sabrina turned back to survey her domain. The Crossroads Diner hummed with the echoes of laughter and conversation, the lingering presence of those who had found solace and connection within its walls.

This is more than just a diner, she thought, a smile playing at the corners of her mouth. *It's a gateway between worlds, a place where the impossible becomes possible. And I'm the lucky one who gets to be at the center of it all.*

Her heart full of gratitude, Sabrina set about preparing for another day of serving up supernatural delights and forging bonds that transcended the boundaries of life and death. The future was uncertain, but one thing was clear: as long as the Crossroads Diner stood, there would always be a place where the living and the dead could come together, united by the power of good food, great company, and a touch of ghostly charm.

Spectres and Souffles

ABOUT THE AUTHOR

      Ladies and gentlemen, step right up to "Where the Magic Happens" - a literary circus that'll make your bookshelf do backflips!
Meet Patti, the ringmaster of this wordy wonderland! She's not just an Executive Producer; she's a word-wrangling wizard, conjuring up an animated TV series based on "ELLIOT FINDS A HOME." It's the tail-wagging tale of a thumbs-up pup and his silent sidekick, proving that you don't need words when you've got opposable digits and a heart of gold!

Hold onto your bestseller lists, folks! This Polygon Entertainment superstar has hit the USA TODAY jackpot and Amazon's #1 spot more times than a cat has lives. With 7 dozen books under her belt, she's got more genres than a chameleon has colors. From Urban Fantasy to Horror, she's been spinning yarns longer than your grandma's knitting needles!

But wait, there's more! Patti's life is like a celebrity bingo card:

She rocked "Romper Room" at 4, probably making the other kids look like amateur rompers.

She rubbed elbows with Captain Kangaroo and Mr. Green Jeans. (No word on whether the jeans were actually green.)

Patti Petrone Miller

She shared a train ride and a sandwich with Sidney Poitier. Talk about a meal ticket to stardom!

She high-fived President Nixon at the circus. Who knew the circus could get any more political?

She went to school with David Copperfield. We assume she didn't disappear during attendance.

She roller-skated with pre-famous John Travolta. Grease lightning, indeed!

She sipped cocoa with Abe Vigoda. Fish never tasted so sweet!

When she's not busy being a literary legend, Patti's juggling roles faster than a circus performer. Teacher, grandma, furparent - she does it all with a smile that could light up a haunted house.

Speaking of haunted houses, meet the "Queen of Halloween" herself! This Wiccan High Priestess is stirring up stories spookier than a skeleton's dance moves. Her books are flying off the shelves faster than witches on broomsticks, so follow her on social media or risk missing out on the hocus-pocus!

So, come one, come all, to Patti's phantasmagorical world of words! It's more exciting than a roller coaster, more magical than a rabbit in a hat, and more diverse than a box of assorted chocolates. Don't be shy - step into the spotlight and join the literary party where the pages turn themselves and the stories never end!